KT-547-752

LUKA AND THE FIRE OF LIFE

Salman Rushdie

Luka and the Fire of Life

JONATHAN CAPE
LONDON

Published by Jonathan Cape 2010

2 4 6 8 10 9 7 5 3 1

Copyright © Salman Rushdie 2010

Salman Rushdie has asserted his right under the Copyright, Designs and
Patents Act 1988 to be identified as the author of this work

First published in Great Britain in 2010 by
Jonathan Cape
Random House, 20 Vauxhall Bridge Road,
London SW1V 2SA

www.rbooks.co.uk

Addresses for companies within The Random House Group Limited can be found at:
www.randomhouse.co.uk/offices.htm

The Random House Group Limited Reg. No. 954009

A CIP catalogue record for this book
is available from the British Library

ISBN 9780224061629 (HARDBACK)
ISBN 9780224090216 (TRADE PAPERBACK)
ISBN 9780224093392 (Waterstones Limited Edition)

The Random House Group Limited supports The Forest Stewardship
Council (FSC), the leading international forest certification organisation. All our
titles that are printed on Greenpeace approved FSC certified paper carry the FSC logo.
Our paper procurement policy can be found at www.rbooks.co.uk/environment

Typeset in Bembo by Palimpsest Book Production Limited,
Falkirk, Stirlingshire

Printed and bound in Great Britain by
Clays Ltd, St Ives plc

M agic lands lie all around,
I nside, outside, underground.
L ooking-glass worlds still abound.
A ll their tales this truth reveal:
N aught but love makes magic real.

1

The Terrible Thing That Happened on the Beautiful Starry Night

There was once, in the city of Kahani in the land of Alifbay, a boy named Luka who had two pets, a bear named Dog and a dog named Bear, which meant that whenever he called out 'Dog!' the bear waddled up amiably on his hind legs, and when he shouted 'Bear!' the dog bounded towards him wagging his tail. Dog the brown bear could be a little gruff and bearish at times, but he was an expert dancer, able to get up on to his hind legs and perform with subtlety and grace the waltz, the polka, the rhumba, the wah-watusi and the twist, as well as dances from nearer home, the pounding bhangra, the twirling *ghoomar* (for which he wore a wide mirror-worked skirt), the warrior dances known as the *spaw* and the *thang-ta*, and the peacock dance of the south. Bear the dog was a chocolate Labrador, and a gentle, friendly dog, though sometimes a bit excitable and nervous; he absolutely could not dance, having, as the saying goes, four left feet, but to make up for his clumsiness he possessed the gift of perfect pitch, so he could sing up a storm, howling out the melodies of the most popular songs of the day, and never going out of tune. Bear the dog and Dog the bear quickly became much more than Luka's pets. They turned into his closest allies and most loyal protectors, so fierce in his defence that nobody would ever have dreamed of bullying him when they were nearby, not even his appalling classmate Ratshit, whose behaviour was usually out of control.

This is how Luka came to have such unusual companions. One fine day when he was twelve years old, the circus came to town — and not just any circus, but the GROF, or Great Rings of Fire, itself, the most celebrated circus in all of Alifbay, 'featuring the Famous Incredible Fire Illusion'. So Luka was at first bitterly disappointed when his father, the storyteller Rashid Khalifa, told him they would not be going to the show. 'Unkind to animals,' Rashid explained. 'Once it may have had its glory days but these days the GROF has fallen far from Grace.' The Lioness had tooth decay, Rashid told Luka, and the Tigress was blind and the Elephants were hungry and the rest of the circus menagerie was just plain miserable. The Ringmaster of the Great Rings of Fire was the terrifying and enormous Captain Aag, aka Grandmaster Flame. The animals were so scared of the crack of his whip that the Lioness with toothache and the blind Tigress continued to jump through hoops and play dead and the skinny Elephants still made Pachyderm Pyramids for fear of angering him, for Aag was a man who was quick to anger and slow to laugh. And even when he put his cigar-smoking head into the Lioness's yawning mouth, she was too scared to bite it off just in case it decided to kill her from inside her belly.

Rashid was walking Luka home from school, wearing, as usual, one of his brightly coloured bush shirts (this one was vermilion) and his beloved, battered panama hat, and listening to the story of Luka's day. Luka had forgotten the name of the tip of South America and had labelled it 'Hawaii' in a geography test. However, he had remembered the name of his country's first president and spelled it correctly in a history test. He had been smacked on the side of the head by Ratshit's hockey stick during games. On the other hand, he had scored two goals in the match and defeated his enemy's team. He had also finally got the hang of snapping his fingers properly, so that they made a satisfying cracking noise. So there were pluses and minuses. Not a bad day overall; but it was about to become a very important day indeed, because this was the day they saw the circus parade going by on its way to raise its Big Top near the banks of the mighty Silsila. The Silsila was the wide, lazy, ugly river with mud-coloured water, which flowed through the city not far from their home. The sight of the droopy cockatoos in their cages and the sad dromedaries humphing along the street touched Luka's generous young heart. But saddest of all, he thought, was the cage in which a mournful dog and a doleful bear stared wretchedly all about. Bringing up the rear of the cavalcade was Captain Aag with his pirate's hard black eyes and his barbarian's untamed beard. All of a sudden Luka became angry (and he was a boy who was slow to anger and quick to laugh). When Grandmaster Flame was right in front of him Luka shouted out at the top of his voice, 'May your animals stop obeying your commands and your rings of fire eat up your stupid tent.'

Now it so happened that the moment when Luka shouted out in anger was one of those rare instants when by some inexplicable accident all the noises of the universe fall silent at the same time, the cars stop honking, the scooters stop phut-phuttering, the birds stop squawking in the trees, and everyone stops talking at once, and in that magical hush Luka's voice rang out as clearly as a gunshot, and his words expanded until they filled the sky, and perhaps even found their way to the invisible home of the Fates who, according to some people, rule the world. Captain Aag winced as if somebody had slapped him on the face and then he stared straight into Luka's eyes, giving him a look of such blazing hatred that the young boy was almost knocked off his feet. Then the world started making its usual racket again, and the circus parade moved on, and Luka and Rashid went home for dinner. But Luka's words were still out there in the air, doing their secret business.

That night it was reported on the TV news that, in an astonishing development, the animals of the GROF circus had unanimously refused to perform. In a crowded tent, and to the amazement of costumed clowns and plain-clothes customers alike, they rebelled against their master in an unprecedented act of defiance. Grandmaster Flame stood in the centre ring of the three Great Rings of Fire bellowing orders and cracking his whip, but when he saw all the animals beginning to walk calmly and slowly towards him, in step, as if they were an army, closing in on him from all directions until they formed an animal circle of rage, his nerve cracked and he fell to his knees, weeping and whimpering and begging for his life. The audience began to boo and throw fruit and cushions, and then harder objects, stones, for example, and walnuts and telephone directories. Aag turned and fled. The animals parted ranks and let him through, and he ran away crying like a baby.

That was the first amazing thing. The second took place later that night. A noise started up around midnight, a noise like the rustling and crackling of a billion autumn leaves, or maybe even a billion billion, a noise that spread all the way from the Big Top by the banks of the Silsila to Luka's bedroom, and woke him up. When he looked out of his bedroom window he saw that the Great Tent was on fire, burning brightly in the field by the river's edge. The Great Rings of Fire were ablaze; and it was not an illusion.

Luka's curse had worked.

The third amazing thing happened the next morning. A dog with a tag on its collar reading 'Bear' and a bear with a tag on its collar reading 'Dog' showed up at Luka's door – afterwards Luka would wonder exactly how they had found their way there – and Dog the bear began to twirl and jig enthusiastically while Bear the dog yowled out a foot-tapping melody. Luka and his father Rashid Khalifa and his mother Soraya and his older brother Haroun gathered at the door of their house to watch, while from her veranda their neighbour, Miss Oneeta, shouted, 'Have a care! When animals begin to sing and dance, then plainly some witchy business is afoot!' But Soraya Khalifa laughed. 'The animals are celebrating their freedom,' she said. Then Rashid adopted a grave expression, and told his wife about Luka's curse. 'It seems to me,' he opined, 'that if any witchy business has been done it is our young Luka who has done it, and these good creatures have come to thank him.'

The other circus animals had escaped into the Wild and were never seen again, but the dog and the bear had plainly come to stay. They had even brought their own snacks. The bear was carrying a bucket of fish and the dog wore a little coat with a pocket full of bones. 'Why not, after all?' cried Rashid Khalifa gaily. 'My storytelling performances could do with a little help. Nothing like a dog-and-bear song-and-dance act to get an audience's attention.' So it was settled, and later that day it was Luka's brother Haroun who had the last word. 'I knew it would happen soon,' he said. 'You've reached the age at which people in this family cross the border into the magical world. It's your turn for an adventure – yes, it's finally here! – and it certainly looks like you've started something now. But be careful. Cursing is a dangerous power. I was never able to do anything so – well – *dark*.'

'*An adventure of my very own*,' Luka thought in wonderment, and his big brother smiled, because he knew perfectly well about Luka's Secret Jealousy, which was actually Not So Secret At All. When Haroun had been Luka's age he had travelled to the Earth's second moon, befriended fishes who spoke in rhyme and a gardener made of lotus roots, and helped to overthrow the evil Cultmaster Khattam-Shud who was trying to destroy the Sea of Stories itself. By contrast, Luka's biggest adventures to date had taken place during the Great Playground Wars at school, in which he had led his gang, the Intergalactic Penguins Team, to a famous victory over the Imperial Highness Army led by his hated rival, Adi Ratshit, aka Red Bottom, winning the day with a daring aerial attack involving paper planes loaded with itching powder. It had been extremely satisfying to watch Ratshit jump into the playground pond to calm down the itch that had spread all over his body; but Luka knew that, compared to Haroun's achievements, his really didn't amount to very much at all. Haroun, for his part, knew about Luka's desire for a real adventure, preferably one involving improbable creatures, travel to other planets (or at least satellites) and P2C2Es, or Processes Too Complicated To Explain. But until now he had always tried to damp down Luka's lusts. 'Be careful what you wish for,' he told Luka, who replied, 'To be honest with you, that is easily the most annoying thing you have ever said.'

In general, however, the two brothers, Haroun and Luka, rarely quarrelled and, in fact, got on unusually well. An eighteen-year age gap had turned out to be a good place to dump most of the problems that can sometimes crop up between brothers, all those little irritations that make the older brother accidentally knock the kid's head against a stone wall or put a pillow over his sleeping face by mistake, or persuade the younger brother that it's a good idea to fill the big fellow's shoes with sweet, sticky mango pickle, or to call the big guy's new girlfriend by a different girlfriend's name and then pretend it was just a really unfortunate slip of the tongue. So none of that happened. Instead, Haroun taught his younger brother many useful things, kick-boxing, for example, and the rules of cricket, and what music was cool and what was not; and Luka uncomplicatedly adored his older brother, and thought he looked like a big bear – a bit like Dog the bear, in fact – or, perhaps, like a comfortable stubbly mountain with a wide grin near the top.

Luka had first amazed people just by getting born, because his brother Haroun was already eighteen years old when his mother Soraya at the age of forty-one gave birth to a second fine young boy. Her husband Rashid was lost for words, and so, as usual, found far too many of them. In Soraya's hospital ward, he picked up his newborn son, cradled him gently in his arms and peppered him with unreasonable questions. 'Who'd have thought it? Where did you come from, buster? How did you get here? What do you have to say for yourself? What's your name? What will you grow up to be? What is it you want?' He had a question for Soraya, too. 'At our age,' he marvelled, shaking his balding head, 'what's the meaning of a wonder like this?' Rashid was fifty years old when Luka arrived, but at that moment he sounded like any young, greenhorn father flummoxed by the arrival of responsibility, and even a little scared.

Soraya took the baby back and calmed its father down. 'His name is Luka,' she said, 'and the meaning of the wonder is that we appear to have brought into the world a fellow who can turn back Time itself, make it flow the wrong way and make us young again.'

Soraya knew what she was talking about. As Luka grew older, his parents seemed to get younger. When baby Luka sat up straight for the first time, for example, his parents became incapable of sitting still. When he began to crawl, they hopped up and down like excited rabbits. When he walked, they jumped for joy. And when he spoke for the first time, well!, you'd have thought the whole of the legendary Torrent of Words had started gushing out of Rashid's mouth, and he was never going to stop spouting on about his son's great achievement.

The Torrent of Words, by the way, thunders down from the Sea of Stories into the Lake of Wisdom, whose waters are illumined by the Dawn of Days, and out of which flows the River

8

of Time. The Lake of Wisdom, as is well known, stands in the shadow of the Mountain of Knowledge at whose summit burns the Fire of Life. This important information regarding the layout – and, in fact, the very existence – of the Magical World was kept hidden for thousands of years, guarded by mysterious, cloaked spoilsports who called themselves the Aalim, or Learned Ones. However, the secret was out now. It had been made available to the general public by Rashid Khalifa in many celebrated tales. So everyone in Kahani was fully aware that there was a World of Magic existing in parallel with our own non-Magic one, and from that Reality came White Magic, Black Magic, dreams, nightmares, stories, lies, dragons, fairies, blue-bearded genies, mechanical mind-reading birds, buried treasure, music, fiction, hope, fear, the gift of eternal life, the angel of death, the angel of love, interruptions, jokes, good ideas, rotten ideas, happy endings, in fact almost everything of any interest at all. The Aalim, whose idea of Knowledge was that it belonged to them and was too precious to be shared with anyone else, probably hated Rashid Khalifa for letting the cat out of the bag.

But it is not yet time to speak – as we will eventually have to speak – of Cats. It is necessary, first of all, to talk about the terrible thing that happened on the beautiful starry night.

Luka grew up left-handed, and it often seemed to him that it was the rest of the world that worked the wrong way around, not him. Doorknobs turned the wrong way, screws insisted on being screwed in clockwise, guitars were strung upside down, and the scripts in which most languages were written ran awkwardly from left to right, except for one, which he bizarrely failed to master. Pottery wheels wheeled perversely, dervishes would have whirled better if they whirled in the opposite direction, and how much finer and more sensible the whole world would be, Luka thought, if the sun rose in the west and set in the east. When he dreamed of life in that Widdershins Dimension, the alternative left-handed Planet Wrongway on which he would be normal instead of unusual, Luka sometimes felt sad. His brother Haroun was right-handed like everyone else, and consequently everything seemed easier for him, which did not seem fair. Soraya told Luka not to be depressed. 'You are a child of many gifts,' she said, 'and maybe you are correct to believe that the left way around is the right way, and that the rest of us are not right, but wrong. Let your hands take you where they will. Just keep them busy, that's all. Go left by all means but don't dawdle; do not be left behind.'

After Luka's curse on the Great Rings of Fire circus worked so spectacularly, Haroun often warned him in a scary voice that his left-handedness might be a sign of dark powers bubbling inside him. 'Just be careful,' Haroun said, 'not to go down the Left-Hand Path.' The Left-Hand Path was apparently the road to Black Magic, but as Luka didn't have the faintest idea how to take that Path even if he wanted to, he dismissed his brother's warning as the kind of thing Haroun sometimes said to tease him, without understanding that Luka did not like to be teased.

Maybe because he dreamed about emigrating to a Left-Handed Dimension, or maybe because his father was a professional storyteller, or maybe because of his brother Haroun's big adventure, or maybe for no reason at all except that that was the way he was, Luka grew up with a strong interest in, and aptitude for, other realities. At school he became so convincing an actor that when he impersonated a hunchback, an emperor, a woman or a god, everyone who watched his performance came away convinced that the young fellow had somehow temporarily grown a hump, ascended a throne, changed sex or become divine. And when he drew and painted, his father's stories of, for example, the elephant-headed Memory Birds who remembered everything that had ever happened, or the Sickfish swimming in the River of Time, or the Land of Lost Childhood, or the Place Where Nobody Lived, came to wonderful, phantasmagoric, richly coloured life. At mathematics and chemistry, unfortunately, he was not so hot. This displeased his mother, who, even though she sang like an angel, had always been the sensible, practical type; but it secretly delighted his father, because for Rashid Khalifa mathematics was as mysterious as Chinese and twice as uninteresting; and, as a boy, Rashid had failed his own chemistry examinations by spilling concentrated sulphuric acid over his practical paper and handing it in full of holes.

Fortunately for Luka, he lived in an age in which an almost infinite number of parallel realities had begun to be sold as toys. Like everyone he knew, he had grown up destroying fleets of invading rocket ships, and been a little plumber on a journey through many bouncing, burning, twisting, bubbling levels to rescue a prissy princess from a monster's castle, and metamorphosed into a zooming hedgehog and a street fighter and a rock star, and stood his ground undaunted in a hooded cloak while a demonic figure with stubby horns and a red-and-black face leapt around him slashing a double-ended light sabre at his head. Like everyone he knew, he had joined imaginary communities in cyberspace, electro-clubs in which he adopted the identity of, for example, an Intergalactic Penguin named after a member of the Beatles, or, later, a completely invented flying being whose height, hair colour and even sex were his to choose and alter as he pleased. Like everyone he knew, Luka possessed a wide assortment of pocket-sized alternate-reality boxes, and spent much of his spare time leaving his own world to enter the rich, colourful, musical, challenging universes inside these boxes, universes in which death was temporary (until you made too many mistakes and it became permanent) and a life was a thing you could win, or save up for, or just be miraculously granted because you happened to bump your head into the right brick, or eat the right mushroom, or pass through the right magic waterfall, and you could store up as many lives as your skill and good fortune could get you. In Luka's room near a small television set stood his most precious possession, the most magical box of all, the one offering the richest, most complex journeys into other-space and different-time, into the zone of multi-life and temporary death: his new Muu. And just as Luka in the school playground had been transformed into the mighty General Luka, vanquisher of the Imperial Highness Army, commander of the dreaded LAF, or Luka Air Force, of paper planes bearing itching-powder bombs, so Luka, when he stepped away from the world of mathematics and chemistry and into the Zone of Muu, felt at home, *at home* in a completely different way to the way in which he felt *at home* in his home, but at home nevertheless; and he became, at least in his own mind, Super-Luka, Grandmaster of the Games.

Once again it was his father Rashid Khalifa who encouraged Luka, and who tried, with comically little skill, to join him on his adventures. Soraya was sniffily unimpressed, and, being a commonsensical woman who distrusted technology, worried that the various magic boxes were emitting invisible beams and rays that would rot her beloved son's mind. Rashid made light of these worries, which made Soraya worry even more. 'No rays! No beams!' Rashid cried. 'But see how well he is developing his hand–eye coordination, and he is solving problems too, answering riddles, surmounting obstacles, rising through levels of difficulty to acquire extraordinary skills.'

'They are useless skills,' Soraya retorted. 'In the real world there are no levels, only difficulties. If he makes a careless mistake in the game he gets another chance. If he makes a careless mistake in a chemistry test he gets a minus mark. Life is tougher than video games. This is what he needs to know, and so, by the way, do you.'

Rashid did not give in. 'Look how his hands move on the controls,' he told her. 'In those worlds left-handedness does not impede him. Amazingly, he is almost ambidextrous.' Soraya snorted with annoyance. 'Have you seen his handwriting?' she said. 'Will his hedgehogs and plumbers help with that? Will his "pisps" and "wees" get him through school? Such names! They sound like going to the bathroom or what.' Rashid began to smile placatingly. 'The term is *consoles*,' he began but Soraya turned on her heel and walked away, waving one hand high above her head. 'Do not speak to me of such things,' she said over her shoulder, speaking in her grandest voice. 'I am in-console-able.'

It was not surprising that Rashid Khalifa was useless on the Muu. For most of his life he had been well known for his fluent tongue, but his hands had, to be frank, always been liabilities. They were awkward, clumsy, butterfingered things. They were, as people said, all thumbs. In the course of their sixty-two years they had dropped numberless things, broken countless more things, fumbled all the things they didn't manage to drop or break, and smudged whatever he wrote. In general, they were anything but handy. If Rashid tried to hammer a nail into a wall, one of his fingers invariably got in the way, and he was always a bit of a baby about the pain. So whenever Rashid offered to lend Soraya a hand, she asked him – a little unkindly – to kindly keep his hands to himself.

But, on the other hand, Luka could remember the time when his father's hands actually came to life.

It was true. When Luka was only a few years old, his father's hands acquired lives and even minds of their own. They had names, too: there was Nobody (the right hand) and Nonsense (the left), and they were mostly obedient and did what Rashid wanted them to, such as waving about in the air when he wanted to make a point (because he liked to talk a lot), or putting food in his mouth at regular intervals (because he liked to eat a lot). They were even willing to wash the part of Rashid he called his bee tee em, which was really extremely obliging of them. But, as Luka quickly discovered, they also had a ticklish will of their own, especially when he was anywhere within reach. Sometimes when the right hand started tickling Luka and he begged, 'Stop, please stop,' his father replied, 'It's not me. In fact, Nobody's tickling you,' and when the left hand joined in and Luka, crying with laughter, protested, 'You are, you are tickling me,' his father replied, 'You know what? That's just Nonsense.'

Lately, however, Rashid's hands had slowed down, and seemed to have gone back to being just hands. In fact, the rest of Rashid was slowing down as well. He walked more slowly than before (though he had never walked quickly), ate more slowly (though not very much more) and, most worryingly of all, talked more slowly (and he had always talked very, very fast). He was slower to smile than he had been, and sometimes, Luka imagined, it seemed that the thoughts were actually slowing down in his father's head. Even the stories he told seemed to move more slowly than they once had, and that was bad for business. 'If he goes on slowing down at this rate,' Luka told himself with alarm, 'then pretty soon he'll completely grind to a halt.' The image of a completely halted father, stuck in mid-sentence, mid-gesture, mid-stride, just frozen to the spot for ever, was a frightening one; but that, it seemed, was the direction in which things were heading, unless something could be done to get Rashid Khalifa back up to speed. So Luka began to think of how a father might be accelerated; where was the pedal to push that would restore his fading zoom? But before he could solve the problem, the terrible thing happened on the beautiful starry night.

One month and one day after the arrival of Dog the bear and Bear the dog at the Khalifa home, the sky arching over the city of Kahani, the River Silsila and the sea beyond was miraculously full of stars, so brilliant with stars, in fact, that even the glumfish in the depths of the water came up for a surprised look and began, against their wishes, to smile (and if you have ever seen a smiling glumfish looking surprised, you will know that it is not a pretty sight). As if by magic the thick stripe of the galaxy itself blazed out of a clear night sky, reminding everyone of how things had been in the old days before human beings dirtied the air and hid the heavens from view. Because of the smog it had become so unusual to see the Milky Way in the city that people called from house to house to tell their neighbours to come out into the street and look. Everyone poured out of their homes and stood with their chins in the air as if the whole neighbourhood was asking to be tickled, and Luka briefly considered being the tickler-in-chief, but then thought better of the idea.

The stars seemed to be dancing up there, to be swirling around in grand and complicated patterns like women at a wedding decked out in their finery, women shining white and green and red with diamonds, emeralds and rubies, brilliant women dancing in the sky, dripping with fiery jewels. And the dance of the stars was mirrored in the city streets; people came out with tambourines and drums and celebrated, as if it were somebody's birthday. Bear and Dog celebrated, too, howling and bouncing, and Haroun and Luka and Soraya and their neighbour, Miss Oneeta, all danced, too. Only Rashid failed to join the party. He sat on the porch and watched, and nobody, not even Luka, could drag him to his feet. 'I feel heavy,' he said. 'My legs feel like coal sacks and my arms feel like logs. It must be that gravity has somehow increased in my vicinity, because

I am being pulled down towards the ground.' Soraya said he was just being a lazy potato, and after a while Luka, too, let his father just sit there eating a banana from a bunch he had bought from a passing vendor while he, Luka, ran about under the carnival of the stars.

The big sky show went on until late at night, and while it lasted it looked like an omen of something good, of the beginning of an unexpectedly good time. But Luka realised soon enough that it had been nothing of the sort. Maybe it had actually been a kind of farewell, a last hurrah, because that was the night that Rashid Khalifa, the legendary storyteller of Kahani, fell asleep with a smile on his face, a banana in his hand and a twinkle on his brow, and did not wake up the next morning. Instead he slept on, snoring softly, with a sweet smile on his lips. He slept all morning, and then all afternoon, and then all night again, and so it went on, morning after morning, afternoon after afternoon, night after night.

Nobody could wake him.

At first Soraya, thinking he was just overtired, went around shushing everybody and telling everyone not to disturb him. But she soon began to worry, and tried to wake him up herself. She spoke to him gently at first, murmuring words of love. Then she stroked his brow, kissed his cheek, and sang a little song. Finally, growing impatient, she tickled him on the soles of his feet, shook him violently by the shoulders, and as a last resort shouted at the top of her voice into his ear. He let out an approving 'mmm' and his smile broadened a little, but he did not wake.

Soraya sat down on the floor beside his bed and buried her

head in her hands. 'What will I do?' she wailed. 'He always was a dreamer, and now he's gone and decided he prefers his dreams to me.'

Soon enough the newspapers got wind of Rashid's condition and journalists came snaking and oiling around the neighbourhood, trying to get the story. Soraya shooed the photographers away, but the story got written just the same. NO MORE BLATHER FROM THE SHAH OF BLAH, the headlines shouted, a little cruelly. NOW HE'S THE SLEEPING BEAUTY, ONLY NOT SO BEAUTIFUL.

When Luka saw his mother crying and his father in the grip of the Big Sleep, he felt as if the world, or a big part of his world, anyway, was coming to an end. All his life he had tried to creep into his parents' bedroom early in the morning and surprise them before they awoke, and every time they had woken up before he reached their bedside. But now Rashid was not waking up and Soraya was really inconsolable, a word which, as Luka knew, in reality had nothing to do with games, even though right at this moment he wished he was inside some other, fictitious version of reality and could press the Exit button to get back to his own life. But there was no Exit button. He was at home, even though home suddenly felt like a very strange and frightening place, with no laughter and, most horrible of all, no Rashid. It felt as if a thing that had been impossible had become possible, a thing that had been unthinkable had become thinkable, and Luka did not want to give that terrifying thing a name.

Doctors came and Soraya took them into the room where Rashid was sleeping and shut the door. Haroun was allowed inside, but Luka had to stay with Miss Oneeta, which he hated, because she gave him too many sweets to eat and pulled his face towards her so that he was lost between her bosoms like a traveller in an unknown valley that smelled of cheap perfume. After a while Haroun came to see him. 'They say they don't know what is wrong with him,' he told Luka. 'He's just sleeping and they can't say why. They have put a drip into his arm because he isn't eating or drinking and needs nourishment. But if he doesn't wake up –'

'He's going to wake up,' Luka shouted. 'He'll be awake any minute now!'

'If he doesn't wake up,' Haroun said, and Luka noticed that Haroun's hands had tightened into fists, and there was a sort of fisty tightness also in his voice, 'then his muscles will deteriorate and his whole body too and then –'

'Then nothing,' Luka interrupted fiercely. 'He's just resting, that's all. He was slowing down and felt heavy and he needed to rest. He's looked after us all his life, to be honest with you, and now he's entitled to take some time off, isn't that right, Oneeta Auntie?'

'Yes, Luka,' said Miss Oneeta, 'that is right, my darling, I am almost completely sure.' And a tear rolled down her cheek.

Then matters got worse.

Luka lay awake in his bed that night, too shocked and unhappy to sleep. Bear the dog was on the bed, too, whiffling and mumbling and lost in a doggy dream, and Dog the bear lay motionless on a straw mat on the floor. But Luka was wide awake. The night sky outside his window was no longer clear, but cloudy and low, as if it were frowning, and thunder grumbled in the distance like the voice of an angry giant. Then Luka heard the sound of beating wings close by, and he jumped out of bed and ran to the window, stuck his head out of it and twisted his neck round to look up towards the sky.

There were seven vultures flying down towards him, wearing ruffs around their necks, like European noblemen in old paintings, or like circus clowns. They were ugly, smelly and mean. The biggest, ugliest, smelliest and meanest vulture settled down on Luka's windowsill, right next to him, as if they were old friends, while the other six hovered just out of reach. Bear the dog woke up and came to the window fast, growling and baring his teeth; Dog the bear leapt up a moment later and towered over Luka, looking as if he wanted to rip the vulture to pieces there and then. 'Wait,' Luka told them, because he had seen something that needed to be investigated. Hanging from the ruff around the Boss Vulture's neck was a little pouch. Luka reached for it; the vulture made no move. Inside the pouch was a scroll of paper, and on the scroll of paper was a message from Captain Aag.

'Dreadful black-tongued child,' the message read, 'disgusting witch-boy, did you imagine I would do nothing in return for what you did to me? Did you think, vile warlock infant, that I could not damage you more grievously than you damaged me? Were you so vain, so foolish, feeble pint-sized maledictor, that you thought you were the only witch in town? Throw out a curse when you can't control it, O incompetent pygmy hexer, and it will come back to smack you in the face. Or, on this occasion, in perhaps an even more satisfying act of revenge, it poleaxes someone you love.'

Luka began to shiver, even though the night was warm. Was

this the truth? Had his burning curse against the circus boss been answered by a sleeping curse on his father? In which case, Luka thought with horror, the Big Sleep was his fault. Not even the arrival in his life of Dog the bear and Bear the dog could make up for the loss of his dad. But on the other hand, he had noticed his father's slowness long before the night of the dancing stars, so maybe this note was just a hideous lie. At any rate he was determined not to let the Boss Vulture see that he was shaken, so in a loud, firm voice, like the one he used in school plays, he said, 'I hate vultures, to be honest with you, and I'm not surprised that you are the only creatures who stayed loyal to that terrible Captain Aag. What an idea, anyway, to have a vulture act in a circus! Just shows you the type of guy he is. This, also,' Luka added, and tore the note to bits under the vulture's cynical beak, 'is the letter of a nasty man, trying to make out that he could make my father ill. He can't make anyone unwell, obviously, but he does make everyone sick.' Then, summoning up all his courage, he shooed the big bird off his windowsill and closed the window.

The vultures flew away in disarray, and Luka collapsed onto his bed, trembling. His dog and his bear nuzzled at him, but he could not be comforted. Rashid was Sleeping, and he, Luka, could not get rid of the notion that he himself – and he alone – was the one who had brought this curse down on his family.

After a sleepless night, Luka got up before dawn and crept into his parents' bedroom, as he had done so often in happier times. There lay his father, Asleep, with tubes running into his arm to feed him, and a monitor showing his heartbeat as a jagged green line. To tell the truth, Rashid didn't look cursed or even sad. He looked . . . *happy*, as if he were dreaming of the stars, dancing with them while he slept, living with them in the sky, and smiling. But looks weren't everything, Luka knew that much; the world was not always what it seemed to be. Soraya was sleeping on the floor, sitting with her back against the wall. Neither parent woke up, as they always used to do when Luka was sneaking towards them. That was depressing. Dragging his feet, Luka made his way back to his own room. Through the window he could see the sky beginning to lighten. Dawn was supposed to cheer people up, but Luka couldn't think of anything to be cheerful about. He went to the window to draw the curtain so that he could at least lie in the dark and rest for a while, and that was when he saw the extraordinary thing.

There was a man standing in the lane outside the Khalifa residence, wearing a familiar vermilion-coloured bush shirt and a recognisably battered panama hat, and plainly watching the house. Luka was just about to call out, and maybe even send Bear and Dog to chase the stranger away, when the man threw back his head and looked him right in the eye.

It was Rashid Khalifa! It was his father, standing out there, saying nothing, but looking wide awake!

But if Rashid was outside in the lane, then who was sleeping in his bed? And if Rashid was sleeping in his bed, then how could he be outside? Luka's head was whirling and his brain had no idea what to think; his feet, however, had started to run. Pursued by his bear and his dog, Luka ran as fast as he could to where his father was waiting for him. He charged down-stairs barefoot, stumbled slightly, took a step to the right, felt oddly giddy for a moment, regained his balance and hurtled on through the front door. This was wonderful, Luka thought. Rashid Khalifa had woken up and somehow slipped outside for a walk. Everything was going to be all right.

2

Nobodaddy

As he ran out of the front door with Dog and Bear, Luka had the strangest feeling: as if they had crossed an invisible boundary; as if a secret level had been unlocked and they had passed through the gateway that allowed them to explore it. He shivered a little, and the bear and the dog shivered, too, although it was not a cold dawn. The colours of the world were strange, the sky too blue, the dirt too brown, the house pinker and greener than normal . . . *and his father was not his father*, not unless Rashid Khalifa had somehow become partly transparent. This Rashid Khalifa looked exactly like the famous Shah of Blah; he was wearing his panama hat and his vermilion bush shirt, and when he walked and talked it became obvious that his voice was Rashid's voice, and the way he moved was an exact copy of the original, too; but this Rashid Khalifa could be seen through, not clearly but murkily, as if he were half real and half a trick of the light. As the first whispers of dawn murmured in the sky above, the figure's transparency became even more obvious. Luka's head began to spin. Had something happened to his father? Was this see-through father some sort of . . . some sort of . . .

'Are you some sort of ghost?' he asked in a weak voice. 'You are certainly something peculiar and surprising, to say the very least.'

'Am I wearing a white sheet? Am I clanking chains? Do I look ghoulish to you?' demanded the phantom dismissively. 'Am I scary? Okay, don't answer that. The truth is that there are no such things as ghosts or spectres and therefore I am not one. And may I point out that right now I am just as surprised as you?'

Bear's hair was standing on end, and Dog was shaking his head in a puzzled way, as if he had just begun to remember something.

'Why are *you* so surprised?' Luka asked, trying to sound confident. 'You're not the one who can see through me, after all.' The see-through Rashid Khalifa came closer and Luka had to force himself not to run away. 'I'm not here for you,' he said. 'So it is, hmm, unusual for you to have crossed over when you're in perfect health. And your dog and bear, too, by the by. The whole thing is exceedingly irregular. The Frontier is not supposed to be this easily ignored.'

'What do you mean?' Luka demanded. 'What Frontier? Who are you here for?' The moment he asked the second question, he knew the answer, and it drove the first question out of his mind. 'Oh,' he said. 'Oh. Then is my father . . . ?'

'Not yet,' said the see-through Rashid. 'But I'm the patient type.'

'Go away,' Luka said. 'You're not wanted around here, Mr . . . what is your name, anyway?'

The see-through Rashid smiled a friendly smile that somehow wasn't entirely friendly. 'I,' he began to explain, in a kindly voice that somehow didn't feel completely kind, 'I am your father's dea—'

'Don't say that word!' Luka shouted.

'The point I'm trying to make, if I may be allowed to continue,' the phantom insisted, 'is that everyone's dea—'

'Don't *say* it!' Luka yelled.

'—is different,' the phantom said. 'No two are alike. Each living being is an individual unlike all others; their lives have unique and personal beginnings, personal and unique middles, and consequently, at the end, it follows that everyone has their own unique and personal dea—'

'Don't!' Luka screamed.

'—and I am your father's, or I will be soon enough, and at that time you will no longer be able to see through me, because then I will be the real thing and he, I'm sorry to say, will no longer be at all.'

'Nobody is going to take my father away,' Luka cried. 'Not even you, Mr – whatever your name is – with your scary tales.'

'Nobody,' said the see-through Rashid. 'Yes, you can call me that. That's who I am. Nobody is going to take your father away: that is exactly right, and I am the Nobody in question. I am your, you might say, Nobodaddy.'

'That's nonsense,' said Luka.

'No, no,' the see-through Rashid corrected him. 'I'm afraid that Nonsense is not involved. You will discover that I am a no-Nonsense kind of guy.'

Luka sat down on the front step of the house and put his head in his hands. *Nobodaddy*. He understood what the see-through Rashid was telling him. As his father faded away, the phantom Rashid would grow stronger, and in the end there would be only this Nobodaddy and no father at all. But he was very sure of one thing: he was not ready to do without a father. He would never be ready for that. The certainty of this knowledge grew in him and gave him strength. There was only one thing for it, he told himself. This, this Nobodaddy had to be stopped, and he had to think of a way to stop him.

'To be fair,' said Nobodaddy, 'and in a spirit of full disclosure, I should repeat that you have already achieved something extra-ordinary − by crossing the line, I mean − so perhaps you are capable of further extraordinary things. Maybe you are even capable of bringing about the thing you are even now dreaming up; maybe − ha ha! − you will succeed in bringing about my destruction. An adversary! How enjoyable! How positively . . . *darling*. I'm *so* excited.'

Luka looked up. 'What do you mean exactly, "crossing the line"?' he asked.

'Here, where you are, is not there, where you were,' explained Nobodaddy, helpfully. 'This, all of this that you see, is not that which you saw before. This lane is not that lane, this house is not that house, and this daddy, as I have explained, is not that one. If the whole of your world took half a step to the right, then it would bump into this world. If it took half a step to the left . . . well, let's not go into that just now. Don't you see how much more brightly coloured everything is here than it is back home? This, you see . . . I shouldn't even tell you, really . . . this is the World of Magic.'

Luka remembered his stumble in the doorway, and his brief but intense feeling of giddiness. Was that when he crossed the line? And had he stumbled to the right or the left? It must have been the right, mustn't it? So this must be the Right-Hand

Path, must it not? But was that the best Path for him? Shouldn't he, as a left-handed person, have stumbled to the left? . . . He realised that he had no idea what he meant. Why was he on any sort of Path at all, and not just in the lane outside his house? Where might such a Path lead, and should he even think of going down it? Should he be thinking about just getting away from this alarming Nobodaddy and finding his way back to the safety of his bedroom? All this talk of Magic was much too much for him.

Of course Luka knew all about the World of Magic. He had grown up hearing about it from his father every day, and he had believed in it, he had even drawn maps and painted pictures of it – the Torrent of Words flowing into the Lake of Wisdom, the Mountain of Knowledge and the Fire of Life, all that stuff; but he hadn't believed in it in the way that he believed in dining tables, or streets, or stomach upsets. It hadn't been real in the way that love was real, or unhappiness, or fear. It was only real in the way that stories were real while you were reading them, or heat mirages before you got too close to them, or dreams while you were dreaming.

'Is this a dream, then?' he wondered, and the see-through Rashid who called himself Nobodaddy nodded slowly in a thoughtful way. 'That would certainly explain the situation,' he replied agreeably. 'Why not put it to the test? If this is indeed a dream, then maybe your dog and your bear would no longer be dumb animals. I know your secret fantasy, you see. You'd like them to be able to talk, wouldn't you? – to speak to you in your own language and tell you their stories. I'm sure they have extremely interesting stories to tell.'

'How do you know that?' asked Luka, shocked, and again the answer arrived in his head as soon as the question was out. 'Oh. You know because my father knows. I talked to my father about it once, and he said he would make up a story about a talking dog and bear.'

'Quite so,' said Nobodaddy calmly. 'Everything that your father has been, and known, and said and done, is slowly crossing over into me. But I mustn't hog the conversation,' he went on. 'I do believe your friends are trying to get your attention.'

Luka looked round and saw to his astonishment that Bear the dog had risen up on his hind legs and was clearing his throat like a tenor at the opera. Then he began to sing – not in barks, howls or dog-yaps this time, but in plain, understandable words. He sang with a slight foreign accent, Luka noticed, as if he were a visitor from another country, but the words were clear enough, although the tale they told was bewildering.

> 'O I am Barak of the It-Barak,
> The Immortal Dog Men of yore,
> Born from the egg of a magic hawk,
> We could sing and fight and love and talk
> And could never, ever be slain.
>
> Yes, I am Barak of the It-Barak,
> A thousand years old and more,
> I ate black pearls and I wed human girls,
> I ruled my world like an earl in curls,
> And I sang with angelic disdain.

And this is the song of the It-Barak,
A thousand years old, it's true,
But we were unmade by a Chinese curse,
Were turned into pooches and pye-dogs and curs,
And the Kingdom of Dogs became quicksand and bogs,
We no longer sang, but could only bark,
And we went on four legs, not two.
Now we go on four legs, not two.'

Then it was the turn of Dog the bear, who also rose up on his hind legs, and folded his paws in front of him like a school-boy at a public-speaking contest. Then he spoke in clear, human language, and his voice sounded remarkably like Luka's brother Haroun's, and Luka almost fell over when he heard it. Nobodaddy saved him by stretching out a protective arm, exactly as if he were the real Rashid Khalifa. 'O mighty pint-sized liberator,' the bear began grandly, but also, it seemed to Luka, a little uncertainly, 'O incomparably cursing child, know that I was not always as you see me now, but the monarch of, um, a northern land of deep woods and shining snow, hidden behind a circular mountain range. My name was not "Dog" then, but, er . . . Artha-Shastra, Prince of Qâf. In that cold, lovely place we danced to keep ourselves warm, and our dances became the stuff of legend, for as we stamped and leapt the brilliance of our spinning wove the air around us into strands of silver and gold, and this became both our treasure and our glory. Yes! To twirl and to whirl was all our delight, and by whirling and twirling we came round right, and our golden land was a place of wonder and our clothes shone like the sun.'

His voice strengthened, as if he had become more certain of the tale he was telling. 'So we prospered,' he went on, 'but we also aroused the envy of our neighbours, and one of them, the giant, bird-headed fairy prince called –' and here Dog the bear stumbled again – 'um . . . ah . . . oh yes, Bulbul Dev, the Ogre King of the East, who sang like a nightingale but danced like an oaf, was the most envious of all. He attacked us with his legion of giants, the . . . the . . . *Thirty Birds*, beaked monsters with spotted bodies, and we, a dancing, golden people, were too innocent and kindly to resist. But we were stubborn folk, too, and we did not give up the secrets of the dance. Yes, yes!' he exclaimed excitedly, and rushed on to the story's end. 'When the Bird Ogres realised that we would not teach them how to spin air into gold, that we would defend that great mystery with our lives, they set up a fluttering and a flapping and a screeching and a cawing so dreadfully terrifying that it was plain that Black Magic was afoot. Within moments the people of Qâf, shattered by the Ogres' shrieks, began to crumble, to lose human form and become dumb animals – donkeys, marmosets, anteaters and, yes, bears – while Bulbul Dev cried, "Try to dance your golden dance now, fools! Try to jig your silver jigs! What you would not share, you have lost for ever, along with your humanity. Low, grubbing animals you will remain, unless – ha ha! – you steal the Fire of Life itself to set you free!" By which he meant, of course, that we would be trapped for ever, for the Fire of Life is no more than a story, and even in stories it is impossible to steal. So I became a bear – a dancing bear, yes, but a golden dancer no more! – and as a bear I wandered the world until Captain Aag caught me for his circus, and so, young master, I found you.'

It was just the sort of story Haroun would have told, thought Luka, a tall tale straight from the great Story Sea. But, when at last it was over, Luka was overcome by a strong feeling of disappointment. 'So you're both people?' he asked regretfully. 'You're not really my bear and my dog, but enchanted princes in dog and bear suits? Am I supposed not to call you "Dog" and "Bear" but "Artha-whatever" and "Barak"? And here I am, worried sick about my dad, and now I'm supposed to worry about how to get you guys turned back into your real selves as well? You do know, I hope, that I'm only twelve years old.'

The bear came back down onto four legs. 'It's okay,' he said. 'While I'm in bear form you can go on calling me "Dog".'

'And while I'm a dog,' said the dog, 'you can still call me "Bear". But it's true that, as long as we are here in the World of Magic, we would like to search for a way of breaking the spells that bind us.'

Nobodaddy clapped his hands. 'Oh, good,' he cried. 'A quest! I do like a quest. And here we have a three-in-one! Because you're on a quest, too, aren't you, young fellow? Of course you are,' he went on before Luka could say a word. 'You want to save your father, of course you do. You want me, your detested Nobodaddy, to fade away, while your father becomes himself again. You want to destroy me, don't you, young fellow? You want to kill me and you don't know how. Except, as a matter of fact, you do know how. You know the name of the only thing in any world, Real or Magical, that can do what you desire. And even if you had forgotten what it was, you have just been reminded by your friend, the talking bear.'

'You mean the Fire of Life,' said Luka. 'That's what you

33

mean, isn't it? The Fire of Life that burns at the top of the Mountain of Knowledge.'

'Bingo! Bullseye! Spot on!' cried Nobodaddy. 'The Towering Inferno, the Third-Degree Burn, the Spontaneous Combustion, the Flame of Flames. Oh, yes.' He actually capered in delight, doing a soft-shoe shuffle with his feet, and juggling with his panama hat. Luka had to admit that this little dance was exactly the sort of thing Rashid Khalifa did when he was a bit too pleased with himself. But it was odder when you could see through the dancer.

'But that's just a story,' said Luka faintly.

'*Just a story?*' echoed Nobodaddy in what sounded like genuine horror. '*Only a tale?* My ears must be deceiving me. Surely, young whippersnapper, you can't have made so foolish a remark. After all, you yourself are a little Drip from the Ocean of Notions, a short Blurt from the Shah of Blah. You of all boys should know that Man is the Storytelling Animal, and that in stories are his identity, his meaning and his lifeblood. Do rats tell tales? Do porpoises have narrative purposes? Do elephants ele-phantasise? You know as well as I do that they do not. Man alone burns with books.'

'But still, the Fire of Life . . . it *is* just a fairy tale,' insisted Dog the bear and Bear the dog, together.

Nobodaddy drew himself up indignantly. 'Do I look,' he demanded, 'like a fairy to you? Do I resemble, perhaps, an elf? Do gossamer wings sprout from my shoulders? Do you see even a *trace* of pixie dust? I tell you now that the Fire of Life is as real as I am, and that only that Unquenchable Blaze will do what you all wish done. It will turn bear into Man and dog into

Dog-Man, and it will also be the End of Me. Luka! You little murderer! Your eyes light up at the very thought! How thrilling! I am amongst assassins! What are we waiting for, then? Are we starting now? Let's be off! Tick, tock! There is no time to lose!'

At this point Luka's feet began to feel as if somebody was gently tickling their soles. Then the silver sun rose above the horizon, and something quite unprecedented began to happen to the neighbourhood, the neighbourhood that wasn't Luka's real neighbourhood, or not quite. Why was the sun silver, for one thing? And why was everything too brightly coloured, too smelly, too noisy? The sweetmeats on the street vendor's barrow at the corner looked like they might taste odd, too. The fact that Luka was able to look at the street vendor's barrow at all was a part of the strange situation, because the barrow was always positioned at the crossroads, just out of sight of his house, and yet here it was, right in front of him, with those oddly coloured, oddly tasting sweetmeats all over it, and those oddly coloured, oddly buzzing flies buzzing oddly all around it. How was this possible? Luka wondered. After all, he hadn't moved a step, and there was the street vendor asleep under the barrow, so the barrow obviously hadn't moved either; and how did the crossroads arrive as well, um, that was to say, how had he arrived at the crossroads?

He needed to think. He remembered the golden rule that one of his schoolteachers, the science master Mr Sherlock, a man with a pipe and a magnifying glass who always dressed too warmly for the climate, had taught him: *eliminate the impossible, and what remains, however improbable, is the truth*. 'But,' thought Luka, 'what do I do when it's the impossible that remains, when the impossible is the only explanation?' He answered his own question according to Mr Sherlock's golden rule. 'Then the impossible must be the truth.' And the impossible explanation, in this case, was that *if he wasn't moving through the world then the world must be moving past him*. He looked down at his ticklish feet. It was true! The ground was slipping along beneath his bare feet, tickling him gently as it went by. Already he had left the street vendor far behind.

He looked at Dog and Bear, who had started behaving as if they were on an ice rink without skates on, slipping and sliding on the moving roadway and making loud, surprised protesting noises. Luka turned to Nobodaddy. 'You're doing this, aren't you?' he accused him, and Nobodaddy widened his eyes, spread his arms, and replied innocently, 'What? Excuse me? Is there a difficulty? I thought we were in a hurry.'

The worst, or maybe the best, thing about Nobodaddy was that he always behaved exactly like Rashid Khalifa. He had Rashid's facial movements and hand gestures and laugh, and he even acted innocent when he knew perfectly well he wasn't, just the way Rashid did when he was clumsy or wrong or planning a special surprise. His voice was Rashid's voice and his wobbly tummy was Rashid's stomach and he was even begin-ning to treat Luka with a spoiling affection that was totally Rashid-like. All his life Luka had known that his mother was the one who laid down the law and had to be handled with care, while Rashid was, quite frankly, a bit soft. Was it possible that Rashid's character had crept into his would-be nemesis, Nobodaddy? Was that why this scary anti-Rashid seemed actually to be trying to help Luka out?

'Okay, stop the world,' Luka commanded Nobodaddy. 'There are some things we need to get absolutely clear before anyone goes anywhere with you.'

He thought he heard, high up and far away, the noise of machinery grinding to a halt with a distant screeching noise, and his feet stopped being tickled, and Dog and Bear stopped sliding about. They had gone quite some distance from home already, and were standing, by chance (or not by chance), on more or less the exact spot where Luka had been on the day he shouted at Captain Aag while he and Rashid were watching the sad parade of the circus animals in their cages. The city was waking up. Smoke rose from roadside canteens where strong, sweet milky tea was being brewed. A few early-rising shop-keepers were taking down their shutters and revealing long narrow caverns filled with fabrics, foodstuffs and pills. A policeman with a long stick yawned as he walked by in dark blue shorts. Cows were still sleeping on the pavement, and so were people, but bicycles and motor scooters were already busying the street. A jam-packed bus went past taking people to the industrial zone, where the sadness factories used to stand. Things had changed in Kahani, and sadness was no longer the city's principal export, as it had been when Luka's brother Haroun was young. The demand for glumfish had fallen away, and people preferred to eat better-tasting produce from further away, the grinning eels of the south, the meat of the northern hope-deer, and, more and more, the vegetarian and non-vegetarian foods available from the Cheery Orchard stores that were opening everywhere you looked. People wanted to feel good even when there wasn't that much to feel good about, and so the sadness factories had been shut down and turned into Obliviums, giant malls where everyone went to dance, shop, pretend and forget. Luka, however, was not in the mood for self-deception. He wanted answers.

'No more mystification,' he said firmly. 'Straight answers to straight questions, please.' Now he had to fight to control his voice, but he succeeded, and fought down the dreadful feelings that were filling his whole body. 'Number one,' he cried, 'who sent you? Where do you come from? Where –' and here Luka paused, because the question was a terrifying one – '. . . when your . . . work . . . is done . . . if it's done, that is . . . which it won't be . . . but if it was done . . . where do you plan to go?'

'That is numbers one, two and three, to be exact,' said Nobodaddy, as, to the watching Luka's horrified astonishment, a strolling cow walked *right through him* and went on about its business, 'but let's not quibble.' Then he thought deeply for a long, silent moment. 'Are you familiar,' he said finally, 'with the Bang?'

'The *Big* Bang?' Luka asked. 'Or some other Bang I don't know about?'

'There was only one Bang,' said Nobodaddy, 'so the adjective *Big* is redundant and meaningless. The Bang would only be Big if there was at least one other Little or Medium-Sized or even Bigger Bang to compare it with, and to differentiate it from.'

Luka didn't want to waste time arguing. 'Yes, I've heard of it,' he said.

'Then tell me,' said Nobodaddy, 'what was there before the Bang?'

Now this was one of those Enormous Questions that Luka

38

had often tried to answer, without having any real success. 'What was it that had gone Bang anyway?' he asked himself. 'And how could everything go off with a Bang if there was nothing there to begin with?' It made his head hurt to think about the Bang and so, of course, he didn't think about it very much.

'I know what the answer is supposed to be,' he said. 'It's supposed to be "Nothing", but I don't really get that, to be honest with you. And anyway,' he added as sternly as he could manage, 'that has nothing to do with the subject under discussion.'

Nobodaddy wagged a finger under his nose. 'On the contrary, young would-be assassin,' he said, 'it has everything to do with it. Because if the whole universe could just explode out of Nothing and then just Be, don't you see that the opposite could also be true? That it's possible to *im*plode and *Un*-Be as well as to *ex*plode and *Be?* That all human beings, Napoleon Bonaparte, for example, or the Emperor Akbar, or Angelina Jolie, or your father, could simply return to Nothing once they're . . . done? In a sort of Little, by which I mean personal, Un-Bang?'

'Un-Bang?' Luka repeated, in some confusion.

'Exactly,' said Nobodaddy. 'Not a spreading out but a closing in.'

'Are you telling me,' Luka said, feeling an anger rise in him, 'that my father is about to implode into Nothing? Is that what you're trying to say?'

Nobodaddy did not answer.

'Then what about life after dea—' Luka began, then stopped himself, slapped himself on the head and rephrased the question. 'What about Paradise?'

Nobodaddy said nothing.

'Are you trying to say that it doesn't exist?' Luka demanded. 'Because if that's what you are trying to say, I know a lot of people in this town who will give you a pretty heated argument.'

Not a word from Nobodaddy.

'You're suddenly very silent,' Luka said crossly. 'Maybe you don't know as many answers as you pretend you do either. Maybe you're not as big a deal as you think.'

'Ignore him,' said Dog the bear in an oddly big-brotherly way. 'You really should go home now.'

'Your mother will be worrying,' said Bear the dog.

Luka was still not used to the animals' new powers of speech. 'I want an answer before I go,' he said stubbornly.

Nobodaddy nodded, slowly, as if a conversation he had been having with someone invisible had just come to an end. 'I can tell you this,' he said. 'That when my work is done, when I have absorbed your father's . . . well, never mind what I will have absorbed,' he added hastily, seeing the look on Luka's face, 'then I – yes, I, myself! – will implode. I will collapse into myself, and simply cease to Be.'

Luka was astounded. 'You? You're the one who's going to die?'

'Un-Be,' Nobodaddy corrected him. 'That's the technical term. And as I have answered your third question first, I should add that, one, nobody sent me, but somebody did send *for* me, and, two, I don't exactly come from somewhere, but I do come from some*one*. And if you think about it for a moment, you will know who that somebody and that someone are, especially as

40

they are one and the same, and I am the spitting image of them Both, who are only One.'

The silver sun brightened in the east. Dog and Bear looked agitated. It was definitely time for Luka to be at home getting ready for the school day. Soraya would be beside herself with worry. Maybe she had sent Haroun out to search the neighbourhood streets. When Luka got home for breakfast he was going to be in nineteen different kinds of trouble. But Luka wasn't thinking about breakfast, or about school. This was not the time for cereal, Ratshit or geography. He was thinking about things he had hardly ever thought about in his life. He was thinking about Life and Dea— well, Un-Life. He still couldn't bear that other, incomplete word.

'And the Fire of Life can save my father,' he said.

'If you can steal it for him,' said Nobodaddy, 'then, yes, without a doubt.'

'And it will give Dog and Bear back their real lives as well.'
'It will.'

'And what will happen to you then? If we succeed?'
Nobodaddy did not reply.

'You won't have to implode, will you? You won't Un-Be.'
'That is so,' Nobodaddy said. 'It won't be my time.'

'So you'll go away.'
'Yes,' said Nobodaddy.

'You'll go away and never come back.'
'"Never" is a long word,' said Nobodaddy.

'Okay . . . but you won't come back for a long time.'
Nobodaddy inclined his head in agreement.

'A long, long time,' Luka insisted.

Nobodaddy pursed his lips and spread out his arms in a kind of surrender.

'A long, long, long –'

'Don't push your luck,' Nobodaddy said sharply.

'And that's why you're trying to help us, isn't it?' Luka concluded. 'You don't want to implode. You're trying to save your own skin.'

'I don't have skin,' said Nobodaddy.

'I don't trust him,' said Bear the dog.

'I don't like him,' said Dog the bear.

'I don't believe a word he says,' said Bear the dog.

'I don't think for one moment that he'll just go away,' said Dog the bear.

'It's a trick,' said Bear the dog.

'It's a trap,' said Dog the bear.

'There's a catch,' said Bear the dog.

'There must be a catch,' said Dog the bear.

'Ask him,' said Bear the dog.

Nobodaddy took off his panama hat, scratched his bald head, lowered his eyes and sighed.

'Yes,' he said. 'There's a catch.'

Actually, there were two catches. The first, according to Nobodaddy, was that *nobody in the entire recorded history of the World of Magic had ever successfully stolen the Fire of Life*, which was protected in so many ways that, according to Nobodaddy, there wasn't enough time to list one-tenth of them. The dangers were almost infinite, the risks dizzying, and only the most fool-hardy adventurer would even think of attempting such a feat.

'It's *never* been done?' Luka asked.

'Never successfully,' Nobodaddy replied.

'What happened to the people who tried?' Luka demanded.

Nobodaddy looked grim. 'You don't want to know,' he said.

'Okay,' said Luka, 'so what's the second catch?'

Darkness fell – not everywhere, but just around Luka, Dog, Bear and their strange companion. It was as if a cloud had covered the sun, except that the sun could still be seen shining in the eastern sky. Nobodaddy seemed to darken, too. The temperature dropped. The noises of the day faded away. Finally Nobodaddy spoke in a low, heavy voice.

'Somebody has to die,' he said.

Luka was angry, confused and frightened all at the same time. 'What do you mean?' he shouted. 'What sort of a catch is that?'

'Once someone like me has been summoned,' said Nobodaddy, 'someone alive must pay for that summons with a life. I'm sorry, but that's the rule.'

'That's a stupid rule, to be honest with you,' said Luka, as powerfully as he could, even though his stomach was churning. 'Who made a stupid rule like that?'

'Who made the Laws of Gravity, or Motion, or Thermo-dynamics?' Nobodaddy asked. 'Maybe you know who discovered them, but that's not the same thing, is it? Who invented Time or Love or Music? Some things just Are, according to their own Principles, and you can't do a thing about it, and neither can I.'

Slowly, slowly, the darkness that had encircled the four of them faded away and the silver sunlight touched their faces.

Luka realised with horror that Nobodaddy wasn't as see-through as he had been before: which could only mean that Rashid Khalifa had grown weaker in his Sleep. That settled it. They didn't have time to waste on chit-chat. 'Will you show me the way to the Mountain?' Luka asked Nobodaddy, who grinned a grin that wasn't at all humorous, and then nodded his head. 'Okay,' said Luka. 'Then let's go.'

3

The Left Bank of the River of Time

The River Silsila was not a beautiful river, in Luka's opinion. Maybe it started out prettily enough up in the mountains somewhere, as a shining, skipping stream rushing over smooth stones, but down here in the coastal plains it had grown fat, lazy and dirty. It slopped from side to side in wide, snaky curves, and it was mostly a pale brown colour, except that in places it looked green and slimy, and then there were purple oil slicks on the surface here and there, and the occasional dead cows floating sadly out to sea. It was a dangerous river, too, because it ran at different speeds; it could accelerate without warning and sweep your boat away, or it could bog you down in a slowly swirling eddy and you would be stuck there for hours, calling uselessly for help. There were treacherous shallows that could maroon you on a sandbank, or sink a large vessel, a ferry boat or a barge, if it hit an underwater rock. There were murky depths in which Luka imagined that almost anything ugly, unclean and glutinous might be living, and certainly there was not, anywhere in all the filthy flow, anything worth catching to eat. If you fell into the Silsila you were supposed to go to the hospital to be cleaned up, and you were given tetanus shots as well.

The only good thing about the river was that over the course of thousands of years it had pushed up high embankments of earth, called Bunds, on both banks, so that it was hidden from view unless you actually climbed up on top of those dykes and looked down at the liquid serpent as it flowed along, and smelled its horrid smell. And thanks to the Bunds the river never flooded, not even in the rainy season when its level rose and rose, so the city was spared the nightmare of that brown, green and purple water full of nameless slimy monsters and dead cattle pouring down into its streets.

The Silsila was a working river; it transported grain and cotton and wood and fuel from the countryside through the city to the sea, but the bargees handling the freight on the long, flat lighters were renowned for their foul tempers; they spoke to you rudely, they shouldered you out of their way on the pavement, and Rashid Khalifa liked to say that the Old Man of the River had cursed them and made them dangerous and bad, like the river itself. The citizens of Kahani tried to ignore the river as much as possible, but now Luka found himself standing right beside its left, that was to say its southern, Bund, wondering how he had arrived there without moving a muscle. Dog the bear and Bear the dog were right beside him, looking as puzzled as he was, and of course Nobodaddy was there, too, grinning his mysterious grin, which looked exactly like Rashid Khalifa's grin, but wasn't.

'What are we doing here?' Luka demanded.

'Your wish was my command,' said Nobodaddy, folding his arms across his chest. ' "Let's go," you said, so we went. Shazam!'

'As if he's some sort of genie from some kind of lamp,' snorted Dog the bear in Haroun's loud voice. 'As if we don't know that the true Wonderful Lamp belongs to Prince Aladdin and his princess, Badr al-Budur, and is therefore not in this place.'

'Um,' said Bear the dog, who was the soft-spoken, practical type, 'how many wishes exactly is he offering? And can anyone wish?'

'He's no genie,' Dog the bear said bearishly. 'Nobody rubbed anything.'

Luka was still puzzled. 'What's the point of coming to the River Stinky, anyway?' he asked. 'It just goes out into the sea, so, to be honest with you, it wouldn't be any use to us even if it wasn't the Stinky, which it is.'

'Are you sure about that?' Nobodaddy asked. 'Don't you want to climb up to the top of the Bund and have a look?'

So Luka climbed, and Dog and Bear climbed with him, and Nobodaddy was somehow waiting at the top when they got there, looking cool as cola on the rocks. But right then Luka wasn't interested in how Nobodaddy got to the top of the Bund because he was looking at something that was literally out of this world. *The river flowing where the stinky Silsila should have been was a completely different river.*

The new river was shining in the silver sunlight, shining like money, like a million mirrors tilted towards the sky, like a new hope. And as Luka looked into the water and saw there the thousand thousand thousand and one different strands of liquid, flowing together, twining around and around one another, flowing in and out of one another, and turning into a different thousand thousand thousand and one strands of liquid, he suddenly understood what he was seeing. It was the same enchanted water his brother, Haroun, had seen in the Ocean of the Streams of Story eighteen years earlier, and it had tumbled down in a Torrent of Words from the Sea of Stories into the Lake of Wisdom and flowed out to meet him. So this was — it had to be — what Rashid Khalifa had called it: the River of Time itself, and the whole history of everything was flowing along before his very eyes, transformed into shining, mingling, multicoloured story streams. He had accidentally taken a stumbling step to the right and entered a World that was not his own, and in this World there was no River Stinky but this miraculous water instead.

He looked in the direction the river was flowing, but a mist sprang up near the horizon and obscured his view. 'I can't see the future, and that feels right,' Luka thought, and turned to look the other way, where the visibility was good for some distance, almost as far as he could see, but the mist was back there, too, he knew that; he had forgotten some of his own past and didn't know that much about the universe's. In front of him flowed the Present, brilliant, mesmerising, and he was so busy staring at it that he didn't see the Old Man of the River until the long-bearded fellow came right up in front of him holding a Terminator, an enormous science-fiction-type blaster, and shot him right in the face.

BLLLAAARRRTT!

It was interesting, Luka thought as he flew apart into a million shiny fragments, that he could still think. He hadn't thought that thinking would be a thing you would be able to do when you had just been disintegrated by a giant science-fiction-type blaster. And now the million shiny fragments had somehow gathered together in a little heap, with Bear the dog and Dog the bear crying out in anguish beside it, and now the million fragments were joining up again, making little shiny sucking noises as they did so, and now – pop! – here he was, back in one piece, himself again, standing on the Bund next to Nobodaddy, who was looking amused, and the Old Man of the River was nowhere to be seen.

'Luckily for you,' said Nobodaddy pensively, 'I gave you a few courtesy lives to start you off. You'd better collect some more before he returns, and you'd better work out what to do about him, too. He's a bad-tempered old man, but there are ways round him. You know how this goes.'

And Luka found that he did know. He looked around him. Dog the bear and Bear the dog had already started work. Bear was digging up the whole neighbourhood, and sure enough there were bones to be found everywhere, little crunchy bones, worth one life, that Bear could grind up and swallow in a trice, and bigger bones that took some hauling out of the earth and quite a lot of crunching up, that were worth between ten and one hundred lives apiece. Meanwhile, Dog the bear was off in the trees lining the Bund, looking for the hundred-life beehives hidden among the branches, and, on the way, swatting down and gobbling up any number of golden, single-life bees. Lives were everywhere, in everything, disguised as stones, vegetables, bushes, insects, flowers, or abandoned candy bars or bottles of pop; a rabbit scurrying in front of you could be a life and so might a feather blowing in the breeze right in front of your nose. Easily found, easily gathered, lives were the small change of this world, and if you lost a few, it didn't matter; there were always more.

Luka began to hunt. He used his favourite tricks. Kicking tree stumps and rustling bushes were always good. Jumping into the air and landing hard on both feet shook lives down from the trees, and even made them tumble, like rain, out of the empty air. Best of all, Luka discovered, was punching the peculiar, round-bottomed, ninepin-like creatures who were hopping idly around the high Strand, the elegant, tree-shaded walkway on top of the Bund. These creatures did not fall over when you kicked them, but wobbled violently from side to side instead, giggling and shrieking with pleasure, and crying out in a kind of ecstasy, 'More! More!' while the lives Luka was looking for scurried out of them like shiny bugs. (When the Punchbottoms had run out of life-bugs, they said mournfully, 'No more, no more,' hung their little heads, and bounced shamefacedly away.)

When the lives Luka found landed on the Bund, they took the form of little golden wheels and immediately began to race away, and Luka had to chase them down, taking care not to fall off the Strand into the Waters of Time. He grabbed lives in great handfuls and stuffed them into his pockets, whereupon, with a little *ting*, they dissolved, and became a part of himself; and this was when he noticed the change in his eyesight. A little three-digit counter had somehow become lodged in the top left-hand corner of his field of vision; it was there, in the same place, no matter where he looked or how hard he rubbed his eyes; and the numbers kept going up as he swallowed, or absorbed, his many lives, making, he was sure, a low whirring noise as they did so. He found that he could accept this new phenomenon easily enough. He would need to be able to keep score, because if he ran out of lives, well, the game would be over, and maybe also that other kind of life, the real one, the one he would need as and when he got back to the real world, where his real father lay asleep, desperately needing his help.

He had collected 315 lives (because of the three-digit counter in the top left of his personal screen, he guessed that the maximum number he could collect was probably 999) when the Old Man of the River came up on to the Strand again, with his Terminator in his hand. Luka looked around panicked for somewhere to hide, and at the same time tried desperately to remember what his father had told him about the Old Man, who, it seemed, was not just one of Rashid Khalifa's inventions after all – or else he was here in the World of Magic *because* Rashid Khalifa had made him up. Luka remembered the way his father told the tale:

> 'The Old Man of the River has a beard like a river,
> It flows right down to his feet.
> He stands on the Strand with a gun in his hand,
> The nastiest Old Man you could meet.'

And here indeed was that very Old Man with his long white river-beard and his enormous blaster, coming out onto the riverbank, climbing up the Bund to the Strand. Luka did his very best to summon back the memory of what else the Shah of Blah had told him about this malevolent river-demon. Something about asking the Old Man questions. No, *riddles*, that was it! Rashid loved riddles; he had tormented Luka with riddles day after day, night after night, year after year, until Luka had become good enough to torment him back. Rashid would sit each evening in his favourite squashy armchair and Luka would jump onto his lap, even though Soraya scolded him, warning that the chair wasn't strong enough to take their combined weight. Luka didn't care, he wanted to sit there, and the chair had never broken, or not yet, anyway, and all that riddling was about to come in handy after all.

Yes! The Old Man of the River was a riddler, that was what Rashid had said about him; he was addicted to riddling the way gamblers were addicted to gambling or drunkards to drink, and that was how to beat him. The problem was how to get close enough to the Old Man to say anything when he had that Terminator in his hand and looked determined to shoot on sight.

Luka dodged from side to side, but the Old Man kept coming right at him, and even though first Bear the dog and then Dog the bear tried to get in the way, a couple of *BLLLAAARRRTT*s blew them to pieces and obliged them to wait until their bodies regrouped; and a moment later, Luka, too, had been blasted again, and had to go through the whole business of flying apart into a million shiny fragments and joining up again, making those little sucking noises, feeling relieved that losing a life wasn't the same thing as dying. Then it was back to life-gathering, but this time Luka had made a note of the exact point on the Bund where the Old Man came into view before he hopped up onto the Strand; and once he was up to six hundred lives he stopped collecting, positioned himself, and waited.

No sooner had the Old Man's head come in to view than Luka yelled at the top of his voice, 'Riddle-me-riddle-me-ree!' Which, he knew from his evenings with Rashid, was the time-honoured way of challenging a riddler to a battle. The Old Man of the River stopped in his tracks, and then a big, nasty smile spread across his face. 'Who calls me?' he said in a cawing cackle of a voice. 'Who thinks he can outplay the Rätselmeister, the Roi des Énigmes, the Pahelian-ka-Padishah, the Lord of the Riddles? – do you know what you risk? – do you understand the wager? – the stakes are high! could not be higher! – look at you, you're nothing, you're a child; I don't even know if I want to face you – no, I won't face you, you are not worthy – oh, very well, if you insist – and if you lose, child, then all your lives are mine – do you understand? – *all your lives are mine*. The final Termination. Here, at the beginning, you will meet your End.'

And this is what Luka could have said in reply, but did not, preferring to remain silent: 'And what you don't understand, you horrible Old Man, is that, in the first place, it's my father who is the Riddle King, and he taught me everything he knew. What you further don't understand is that our riddle battles went on for hours and days and weeks and months and years, and therefore I have a supply of tough brain-twisters that will never run out. And what you don't understand most of all is that I've worked out something important, namely that this World I'm in, this World of Magic, is *not just any old Magical*

World, but the one my father created. And because this is *his* Magic World and nobody else's, I know secrets about everything in it, including, O terrible Old Man, about you.'

What he actually said aloud was this: 'And if you lose, Old Man, then you will have to Terminate yourself, not just temporarily, but once and for all.'

How the Old Man laughed! He guffawed until he wept, not only from his eyes but through his nose as well. He held his sides and leapt from side to side, and his long white beard cracked in the air like a whip. 'That's a good one,' he said finally, panting for breath. '*If I lose*. That's priceless. Let's begin.' But Luka wasn't going to be fooled that easily. Riddlers are tricksters, he knew that much, and you had to nail down the deal before you began the battle, or they would try to wriggle out of it later on. 'And if you lose, you will do as I have said,' he insisted. The Old Man of the River made a peevish face. 'Yes, yes, yes,' he replied. 'If I lose I will Self-Terminate. Auto-Terminate. Termination of Me by Me will Occur. Hee, hee, hee. I'll blast myself to bits.' 'Permanently,' Luka said firmly. 'Once and for all.' The Old Man grew serious and his face coloured unpleasantly. 'Very well,' he barked. 'Yes. Permanent Termination if I lose; in a word, *Permination*! But as you are about to discover, child, I'm not the one who is about to lose all his lives.'

Bear and Dog were in a state of high agitation, but now Luka and the Old Man were circling each other, staring each other down, and it was the Old Man who spoke first, in a hard greedy voice pushing roughly through teeth that seemed hungry to eat up little Luka's life.

'What goes round and round the wood but never goes into it?'

'The bark of the tree,' said Luka at once, and shot back, 'It stands on one leg with its heart in its head.'

'Cabbage,' snapped the Old Man. 'What is it that you can keep after giving it to someone else?'

'Your word. I have a little house and I live in it alone. It has no doors or windows, and to go out I must break through the wall.'

'Egg. What do you call a fish without an eye?'

'A fsh. What do sea monsters eat?'

'Fish and ships. Why was six afraid of seven?'

'Because seven eight nine. What has been there for millions of years but is never more than a month old?'

'The moon. When you don't know what it is then it's something, but when you know what it is then it's nothing.'

'That's easy,' Luka said, badly out of breath. 'A riddle.'

They had been circling faster and faster, and the riddles had been coming at greater and greater speed. This was just the beginning, Luka knew; soon the number riddles would start, and the story riddles. The difficult stuff still lay ahead. He wasn't sure if he could last the course, so the thing was not to let the Old Man dictate the pace and manner of the contest. It was time to play the joker in the pack.

He stopped circling and put on his grimmest expression. 'What,' he asked, 'goes on four legs in the morning, two legs at noon, and three legs in the evening?'

The Old Man of the River stopped circling, too, and for the first time there was a weakness in his voice and a tremble in his limbs. 'What are you playing at?' he demanded feebly. 'That's the most famous riddle in the world.'

'Yes, it is,' said Luka, 'but you're stalling for time. Answer me.'

'Four legs, two legs, three legs,' said the Old Man of the River. 'Everyone knows this one. Ha! It's the Oldest One in the Book.'

('The she-monster known as the Sphinx,' Rashid Khalifa used to tell Luka, 'sat outside the city of Thebes and challenged all the travellers who passed by to solve her riddle. When they failed, she killed them. Then one day a hero came by and knew the answer.' 'And what did the Sphinx do then?' Luka asked his father. 'She destroyed herself,' Rashid replied.

'And what was the answer to the riddle?' Luka asked. But Rashid Khalifa had to admit that, no matter how many times he learned the blasted story, he could never remember the solution to the riddle. 'So that old Sphinx,' he said, not very sadly, 'she'd have eaten me up for sure.')

'Come on,' Luka said to the Old Man of the River. 'Your time's up.'

The Old Man of the River looked around in panic. 'I could just blast you anyway,' he said.

Luka shook his head. 'You know you can't do that,' he said. 'Not now. Not any more.' Then Luka allowed his expression to become a little dreamy. 'My father could never remember the answer, either,' he said. 'And this is my father's World of Magic, and you are his Riddle Man. So you can't know what he couldn't recall. And now you and the Sphinx must share the same fate.'

'Permination,' the Old Man of the River said softly. 'Yes. That is just.' And without more ado, and quite unsentimentally, he lifted his Terminator, set the dial on maximum, pointed the weapon at himself, and fired.

'The answer is a man,' Luka said to the empty air, as the tiny, shining smithereens of the Old Man blew away into nothingness, 'who crawls on all fours as a baby, walks upright as a grown-up, and uses a stick when he's old. That's the answer: a man. Everyone knows that.'

The departure of the Gatekeeper at once unveiled the Gate. A trellised stone archway wreathed in bougainvillea flowers magically appeared on the edge of the Bund, and beyond it Luka could see an elegant flight of stairs leading down to the river's edge. There was a golden button set in the archway's left pillar. 'I'd push that if I were you,' suggested Nobodaddy. 'Why?' Luka asked. 'Is it like ringing a doorbell to be invited in?' Nobodaddy shook his head. 'No,' he said patiently. 'It's like saving your progress so that the next time you lose a life you don't have to come back here and fight the Old Man of the River all over again. He may not fall for your little trick next time, either.' Feeling a little stupid, Luka pushed the button, and there was a little answering piece of music, the flowers around the archway grew larger and more colourful, and a new counter appeared in Luka's field of vision, this time in the top right-hand corner, a single-digit counter, reading '1'. He wondered how many levels he would have to surmount, but after his foolishness about the Save button, he decided this was not the moment to ask.

Nobodaddy led the boy, the dog and the bear down the Bund to the left bank of the River of Time. Punchbottoms bounced up towards the travellers, hoping to be kicked – 'Ooch! Ouch! Ooch!' they squeaked in happy anticipation – but everyone's attention was elsewhere. Bear and Dog were both talking at once at the tops of their new voices, half excited, half terrified by Luka's battle against, and victory over, the Old Man of the River, and there were so many *how*s and *what*s and *wow*s and *eek*s in their chatter that Luka couldn't begin to reply. And anyway, he was exhausted. 'I need to sit down,' he said, and his legs gave way beneath him. He landed with a thump in the riverside dust, and it rose up around him in a little golden cloud, which quickly formed itself into a creature, like a tiny living flame with wings. 'Feed me and I live,' it said hotly. 'Give me water and I die.'

The answer was obvious. 'Fire,' Luka said quietly, and the Fire Bug grew agitated. 'Don't say that!' it buzzed. 'If you go shouting *fire* at the top of your voice somebody will probably come running with a hose. Too much water around here for my liking anyway. Time to be off.' 'But wait a minute,' Luka said, excited in spite of being so tired. 'Maybe you're what I've been looking for. Your light is so beautiful,' he added, thinking that a little flattery might not hurt. 'Are you . . . is this . . . could you be part of . . . a bearer of . . . the Fire of Life?'

'Don't mention that,' said Nobodaddy quickly, but it was too late.

'How do you know about the Fire of Life?' the Fire Bug wanted to know, becoming cross. Then it turned its displeasure upon Nobodaddy. 'And you, sir, as far as I can see you should be somewhere else entirely, with something else entirely to do.'

'As you see,' Nobodaddy said to Luka, 'Fire Bugs' temperament is, well, a little heated. Nevertheless, they do perform a minor, useful function, spreading warmth wherever they go.'

The Fire Bug flared up at that. 'You want to know what bugs me?' it said indignantly. 'Nobody's friendly about fire. Oh, it's fine in its place, people say, it makes a nice glow in a room, but keep an eye on it in case it gets out of control, and always put it out before you leave. Never mind how much it's needed; a few forests burned by wildfires, the occasional volcanic eruption, and there goes our reputation. Water, on the other hand! – hah! – there's no limit to the praise Water gets. Floods, rains, burst pipes, they make no difference. Water is everyone's favourite. And when they call it the Fountain of Life! – bah! – well, that just bugs me to bits.' The Fire Bug dissolved briefly into a little cloud of angry, buzzing sparks, then came together again. 'Fountain of Life, indeed,' it hissed. 'What an idea. Life is not a drip. Life is a flame. What do you imagine the *sun* is made of? *Raindrops?* I don't think so. Life is not wet, young man. Life *burns.*'

'We must be going now,' Nobodaddy interjected, ushering Luka, Bear and Dog along the riverbank. To the Fire Bug he said, politely, 'Farewell, bright spirit.'

'Not so fast,' the Fire Bug blazed. 'I sense something smouldering here, under the surface. Somebody here, namely that individual there –' and it pointed a little finger of flame at Luka – 'said something about a certain Fire whose very existence is supposed to be a Secret, and somebody else here, namely myself, wants to know how this other Somebody found out about it, and what this Somebody's plans might be.'

Nobodaddy placed himself between Luka and the Bug. 'That will do, you Insignificant Inflammation,' he said in an altogether sterner voice. 'Be off with you! Sizzle till you fizzle!' He took off his panama hat and waved it in the incandescent insect's direction. The Fire Bug flared up, offended. 'Don't trifle with me,' it cried. 'Don't you know you're playing with Fire?' Then it burst into a bright cloud, singed Luka's eyebrows slightly, and vanished.

'Well, that hasn't made things any easier,' said Nobodaddy. 'All we need is for that dratted Bug to raise the Fire Alarm.'

'The Fire Alarm?' asked Luka. Nobodaddy shook his head. 'If they know you're coming, your goose is cooked, that's all.'

'That's not good,' said Luka, looking so dejected that Nobodaddy actually put an arm around his shoulder. 'The better news is that Fire Bugs don't last long,' he consoled the young fellow. 'They blaze brightly, but they burn out young. Also, they blow with the wind. This way, that way; it's in their nature. No constancy of purpose. So it isn't very likely that he'd make it all the way to warn,' and here Nobodaddy's voice trailed off into silence.

'To warn whom?' Luka insisted.

'The forces that must not be warned,' Nobodaddy replied. 'The flame-breathing monsters and fire-starter maniacs who wait upriver. The ones you have to get past, or be destroyed.'

'Oh,' said Luka bitterly. 'Is that all? I thought you meant there might be a serious problem.'

The River of Time, which had been flowing silently along when Luka first set eyes on it, was now bustling with activity. All manner of strange creatures seemed to be afloat upon it and bobbing up from below the surface – strange, but familiar to Luka from his father's stories: long, fat, blind, whitish Worms who, as Nobodaddy reminded him, were capable of making

Holes in the very fabric of Time itself, diving below the surface of the Present to re-emerge at an impossibly distant point in the Past or Future, those mist-shrouded zones which Luka's gaze could not penetrate; and pale, deadly Sickfish, who fed upon the lifelines of the diseased.

Running along the bank was a white rabbit wearing a waistcoat and looking worriedly at a clock. Appearing and disappearing at various points on both banks was a dark blue British police telephone booth, out of which a perplexed-looking man holding a screwdriver would periodically emerge. A group of dwarf bandits could be seen disappearing into a hole in the sky. 'Time travellers,' said Nobodaddy in a voice of gentle disgust. 'They're everywhere these days.'

In the middle of the river all sorts of bizarre contraptions – some with bat-like wings that didn't seem to fly, others with giant metal machineries aboard like the innards of an old Swiss watch – were circling uselessly, to the rage of the men and women aboard them. 'Time machines are not as easily built as people seem to think,' Nobodaddy explained. 'As a result many of those would-be intrepid explorers just get stuck in Time. Also, on account of the odd relationship between Time and Space, the people who do manage to time-jump sometimes space-jump at the same time and end up' – and here his voice grew darkly disapproving – 'in places where they simply don't belong. Over there, for example,' he said as a raucous DeLorean sports car roared into view from nowhere, 'is that crazy American professor who can't seem to stay put in one time, and, I must say, there is an absolute plague of killer robots from the Future being sent to change the Past. Sleeping there under that banyan tree' – he jerked a thumb to indicate which tree he meant – 'is a certain Hank Morgan of Hartford, Connecticut, who was accidentally transported one day back to King Arthur's Court, and stayed there until the wizard Merlin put him to sleep for thirteen hundred years. He was supposed to wake up back in his own time, but look at the lazy fellow! He's still snoring away, and has missed his Slot. Goodness knows how he will get home now.'

Luka noticed that Nobodaddy was not as transparent as he had been a while earlier, and also that he was sounding and acting more and more like the over-talkative Rashid Khalifa, whose head was always full of all sorts of nonsense. '*Time,*' he was singing under his breath, '*like an ever-rolling stream, bears all its sons away . . .*' That did it. That was all Luka was prepared to hear. As if it wasn't bad enough that this, this creature from the Nether World was slowly filling up with more and more of his beloved father, which meant, of course, that Rashid Khalifa, Asleep in his bed at home, was getting emptier and emptier; and that as Nobodaddy's Rashid-ness increased Luka was confusingly filled with emotions of fondness for him, even of love; but now the strange entity in his father's vermilion bush shirt and panama hat had actually started singing in Rashid's unbearable singing voice, the second-worst singing voice in the known world, second only to the fabled tuneless tones of Princess Batcheat of Gup. And what a song to choose! '*They fly forgotten, as a dream –*'

'We're wasting Time,' Luka interrupted Nobodaddy angrily. 'Instead of singing that stupid hymn, how about suggesting a way for us to travel up into the Fog of the Past and find what we're here to find ... i.e. the Dawn of Time, the Lake of Wisdom, the Mountain of Knowledge, and the —'

'Shh,' said Bear the dog and Dog the bear together. 'Don't say it aloud.' Luka flushed a deep red at his near-mistake. 'You know what I mean,' he finished, much less commandingly than he had intended.

'Hmm,' said Nobodaddy thoughtfully. 'Why don't we use, for example, that incredibly powerful-looking, off-the-road-worthy, river-worthy, strong-as-a-tank, and possibly even jet-propelled, eight-wheeled-slash-flat-bottomed amphibian vehicle moored to that little pier over there?'

'That wasn't there a minute ago,' said Dog the bear.

'I don't know how he did it,' said Bear the dog, 'but I don't like the look of it.'

Luka knew that he couldn't afford to pay attention to his friends' worries, and marched down to the enormous craft, whose name, written in bold letters on the stern, was the *Argo*. His father was fading as Nobodaddy solidified, and as a result the quest had become even more urgent than before. Luka's head was full of questions to which he did not know the answers, difficult questions about the nature of Time itself. If Time was a River, eternally flowing — and here it was, here was the River of Time! — did that mean that the Past would always be there and the Future, too, already existed? True, he couldn't see them, because they were wreathed in mists — which could also be clouds, or fog, or smoke — but surely they had to be there, otherwise how could the River exist? But on the other hand, if Time flowed like a River, then surely the Past would have flowed away already, in which case how could he go back into it to find the Fire of Life which burned in the Mountain of Knowledge which stood by the Lake of Wisdom which was illumined by the Dawn of Days? And if the Past had flowed away, then what was back there at the River's source? And if the Future already existed, then perhaps it didn't matter what he, Luka, did next, because no matter how hard he was trying to save his father's life, maybe Rashid Khalifa's fate had already been decided. But if the Future could be shaped, in part, by his own actions, then would the River change its course depending on what he did? What would happen to the story streams it contained? Would they start telling different stories? And which was true: (a) that people made history, and the River of Time in the World of Magic recorded their achievements, or (b) that the River made history, and people in the Real World were pawns in its eternal game? Which World was more real? Who was finally in charge? Oh, and one more question, maybe the most pressing one of all: *how was he going to control the* Argo? He was a twelve-year-old boy who had never driven a car or stood at the helm of a motorboat; and Dog and Bear were no use, and Nobodaddy had stretched out on the deck, put his panama hat over his face, and closed his eyes.

'Okay,' thought Luka grimly, 'how hard can it be?' He stared at the instruments on the bridge. There was this switch, which probably put the wheels down for driving on when the *Argo* was on land, or up when the *Argo* hit the water; and this button, which was pretty obviously green for 'go', and this one next to it, which was just as self-evidently red for 'stop'; and this lever, which he should probably push forward to go forward, and maybe push further forward to go faster; and this wheel, which would do the steering; and all those dials and counters and needles and gauges, which he could probably just ignore.

'Hold on, everybody,' he announced. 'Here goes.'

Something then happened so rapidly that Luka was not entirely sure how or what it was, but an instant later the jet-propelled amphibian craft was flipping over and over in the middle of the great waterway and then they were all in the water and a whirlpool was sucking them down and Luka just had time to wonder whether he was about to be eaten by a Sickfish or other watery beast when he lost consciousness, and woke up a moment later back at the little pier, climbing into the *Argo*, thinking 'How hard can it be?' – and the only sign that something had happened was that the counter in the top left-hand corner of his field of vision had gone down by one life: 998. Nobodaddy was snoozing on the deck of the *Argo* again, and Luka called out, 'A little help?' But Nobodaddy didn't move, and Luka understood this was something he would have to work out for himself. Perhaps those dials and gauges were more important than he had thought.

On the second try he managed not to turn the *Argo* over, but he didn't get far before the whirlpool started up and whirled the craft around and around. 'What's happening?' Luka yelled, and Nobodaddy lifted his panama hat and replied, 'It's probably the Eddies.' But what were the Eddies? The *Argo* was spinning faster and faster, and in a minute it would be sucked down again. Nobodaddy sat up. 'Hmm,' he said. 'Yes. The Eddies are definitely in the neighbourhood.' He looked down into the water, cupped his hands around his mouth, and shouted, 'Nelson! Duane! Fisher! Stop playing now! Go torment somebody else!' But then the *Argo* was pulled underwater, and there was the blackout again, and they were back at the pier with the counter at 997. 'Fish,' said Nobodaddy briefly. 'Eddyfish. Small, speedy rogues. Causing whirlpools is their favourite sport.' 'And what's to be done about them?' Luka wanted to know. 'You have to work out how it is,' Nobodaddy said, 'that people manage to reach back into the Past.'

'I guess . . . by remembering it?' Luka offered. 'By not forgetting it?'

'Very good,' said Nobodaddy. 'And who is it that never forgets?'

'An elephant,' said Luka, and that's when his eye fell upon a pair of absurd creatures with duck-like bodies and large elephant heads who were bobbing about in the water not far from the *Argo*'s mooring. 'And,' he said slowly, remembering, 'here in the World of Magic, an Elephant Bird as well.'

'Full marks,' Nobodaddy replied. 'The Elephant Birds spend their lives drinking from the River of Time; nobody's memories are longer than theirs. And if you want to travel up the River, Memory is the fuel you need. Jet propulsion will do you no good at all.'

'Can they take us as far as the Fire of Life?' Luka asked.

'No,' said Nobodaddy. 'Memory will only get you so far, and no further. But a long Memory will get you a long way.'

It would be difficult, Luka realised, to ride on the Elephant Birds the way his brother Haroun had once ridden on a big, telepathic, mechanical hoopoe; for one thing, he wasn't sure that Bear and Dog would be able to hold on. 'Excuse me, Elephant Birds,' he called out, 'would you be so good as to help us, please?'

'Excellent manners,' said the larger of the two Elephant Birds. 'That always makes such a difference.' He had a deep, majestic voice; obviously an Elephant Drake, Luka thought. 'We can't fly, you know,' said the Drake's companion in ladylike tones. 'Don't ask us to fly you anywhere. Our heads are too heavy.'

'That must be because you remember so much,' Luka said, and the Elephant Duck preened her feathers with the tip of her trunk. 'He's a flatterer, too,' she said. 'Quite the little charmer.'

'You'll be wanting us to tow you upriver, no doubt,' said the Elephant Drake.

'You needn't look so surprised,' said the Elephant Duck. 'We do follow the news, you know. We do try to keep up.'

'It's probably a good thing they don't bother with the Present where you're going,' added the Elephant Drake. 'Up there they only interest themselves in Eternity. This may give you a helpful element of surprise.'

'And if I may say so,' said the Elephant Duck, 'you're going to need all the help you can get.'

A short while later the two Elephant Birds had been harnessed to the *Argo* and began pulling it smoothly upstream. 'What about the Eddies?' Luka wondered. 'Oh,' said the Elephant Drake, 'no Eddyfish would dare trifle with us. It would be against the natural order of things. There is a natural order of things, you know.' His companion giggled. 'What he means,' she explained to Luka, 'is that we eat Eddyfish for breakfast.' 'And lunch and dinner,' said the Elephant Drake. 'So they give us a wide berth. Now then: where was it you wanted to go? – No, no, don't remind me! – Ah, yes, now I recall.'

4

The Insultana of Ott

The Mists of Time were getting closer when the *Argo* passed
a strange, sad land on the River's right bank. Its territory was
barred to River travellers by high barbed-wire fences, and
when Luka did finally see a scary-looking border post, with its
floodlights on high pylons and its tall reconnaissance towers
containing lookout guards wearing mirrored sunglasses and
carrying powerful military binoculars and automatic weapons, he
was struck by a large sign reading YOU ARE AT THE FRONTIER
OF THE RESPECTORATE OF I. MIND YOUR MANNERS. 'What kind
of a place is this?' he asked Nobodaddy. 'It doesn't look very
Magical to me.'

Nobodaddy's expression contained a familiar mixture of
amusement and scorn. 'I'm sorry to say that the World of Magic
is not immune to Infestations,' he said. 'And this part of it has
been overrun, in recent times, by Rats.'

'Rats?' Luka cried in alarm, and now he realised what was
wrong with those lookouts and border guards. They weren't people
at all, but giant rodents! Dog the bear growled angrily, but Bear
the dog, who was a gentle-hearted soul, looked upset. 'Let's move

on,' he suggested quietly, but Luka shook his head. 'I don't know about anyone else, but I'm starving,' he said. 'Rats or no Rats, we have to go ashore, because we all need something to eat. Well, all of us except you,' he added to Nobodaddy in an aside. Nobodaddy shrugged Rashid Khalifa's familiar shrug and smiled Rashid Khalifa's familiar smile and said, 'Very well, if we must, we must. It's been a while since I passed through the O-Fence.' He saw Luka's frown and explained, 'This barbed-wire contraption. The O-Fence goes all around the Respectorate of I – it gives the place, you could say, its I-dentity – and, as the sign warns you, many of its present occupants take Offence very sharply indeed.'

'We don't plan to be rude,' Luka said. 'We just want lunch.'

The four travellers entered the border post, leaving the *Argo* in the care of the Elephant Drake and Elephant Duck, who passed the time diving for Eddyfish and other morsels. Inside the border post, standing at a counter behind a locked metal grille, was a large grey Rat in uniform: a Border Rat. 'Papers,' it said in a squeaky, Ratty voice. 'We don't have any papers,' Luka honestly replied. The Border Rat went into a frenzy of screeches and squawks. 'Absurd!' it finally yelled. 'Everybody has papers of some sort. Turn out your pockets.' And so Luka emptied his pockets and found there, among the usual clutter of marbles, swap cards, elastic bands and game chips, three sweets still in their wrappers and two small, folded paper airplanes. 'I never heard anything so rude,' the Border Rat cried. 'First he says he has no papers. Then it turns out he has papers. You're lucky I'm the understanding kind. Hand over your papers and be grateful I'm in such a good mood.' Nobodaddy nudged Luka, who regretfully handed over the swap cards, the airplanes and the orange sweets in their transparent wrapping. 'Will that do?' he asked.' 'Only because I'm the forgiving type,' the Border Rat replied, pocketing the objects carefully. He unlocked the grille and allowed the travellers to pass through to the other side. 'A word of warning,' he said. 'Here in the Respectorate we expect visitors to behave. We're very thin-skinned. If you prick us, we bleed, and then we make you bleed double: is that clear?'

'Absolutely clear,' said Luka politely.

'Absolutely clear what?' the Border Rat screeched.

'Absolutely clear, *sir*,' Nobodaddy answered. 'Don't worry, sir. We will most definitely mind our p's and q's. Sir.'

'What about the other twenty-four letters of the alphabet?' asked the Border Rat. 'You can do a lot of damage with those, and never use a q or a p.'

'We'll mind the other letters also,' said Luka, adding, quickly, 'sir.'

'Are any of you female?' the Border Rat abruptly demanded. 'That dog, is she a bitch? That bear, is she a . . . bearess? A bearina? A bearette?'

'Bearina indeed,' said Dog the bear. 'Now I'm the one that's offended.'

'And I,' said Bear the dog. 'Not that I have anything against bitches.'

'The nerve!' squeaked the Border Rat. 'That you say you are offended, insults me mortally. And if you insult one Rat mortally, you offend all Rats gravely. And a grave offence to all Rats is a funeral crime, a crime punishable by –'

'We apologise, sir,' said Nobodaddy hurriedly. 'May we go now?'

'Oh, very well,' said the Border Rat, subsiding. 'But mind your manners. I don't want to have to send for the Respecto-Rats.' Luka didn't like the sound of those.

They came through the border post and found themselves in a grey street: the houses, the curtains at the windows, the clothing worn by Rats and people alike (yes, there were people here, Luka was relieved to see), all grey. The Rats were grey too and the people had acquired a greyish pallor. Overhead, grey clouds allowed a neutral sunlight to filter through. 'They developed a Colour Problem here a little while ago,' Nobodaddy said. 'The Rats who hated the colour yellow because of its, well, cheesiness were confronted by the Rats who disliked the colour red because of its similarity to blood. In the end all colours, being offensive to someone or other, were banned by the Rathouse – that's the parliament, by the way, although nobody votes for it, it votes for itself, and it basically does what the Over-Rat says.'

'And who chooses the Over-Rat?' Luka asked.

'He chooses himself,' said Nobodaddy. 'Actually he chooses himself over and over again, he does it more or less every day, because he likes doing it so much. It's known as being Over-Rat-ed.'

'Overrated sounds about right,' said Dog the bear with a snort, and a number of passing Rats looked round sharply. 'Be careful,' Nobodaddy warned. 'Everyone's looking for trouble around here.'

Just then Luka caught sight of a giant billboard bearing a much-larger-than-life black-and-white portrait of what could only be the Over-Rat in person. 'Oh, my goodness,' he said, because the thought struck him that if the Over-Rat ever turned into a human being – if the Over-Rat could be reincarnated as a horrible twelve-year-old schoolboy from Kahani, to be precise – then he would look exactly like . . . that is, really *exactly like* . . .

'Ratshit,' Luka whispered. 'But it's impossible.' Bear the dog stared at the billboard as well. 'I see what you mean,' he said. 'Let's just hope he's not your enemy in the Magic World as well.'

Here was a place to eat! The sign over the door read *ALICE'S RESTAU-RAT*, which was, unfortunately, not a spelling mistake. Luka looked through the window and was reassured to see that the cooks and staff were all people, though many of the guests were Rats. He was worried, though. How would he and his friends pay for their food? 'Don't fret about that,' Nobodaddy said. 'There's no money in the World of Magic.'

Luka was relieved. 'But then how does anyone, well, buy anything? How do things work? It's very odd.' Nobodaddy gave Rashid Khalifa's shrug again. 'It's,' he replied in his own, mysterious fashion, 'a P2C2E.' A surge of excitement coursed through Luka's body. 'I know what that is,' he said. 'My brother told me. They had those on his adventure, too.'

'Processes Too Complicated To Explain,' said Nobodaddy, a little too grandly, as he led the way into the Restau-Rat, 'are at the heart of the Mystery of Life. They are everywhere, in the Real World as well as the Magical One. Nothing anywhere would work without them. Don't get so excited, Professor. You look like you just discovered Electricity, or China, or Pythagoras' Theorem.'

'Sometimes,' Luka replied, 'it's obvious that you aren't my father.'

★   ★   ★

The food was surprisingly tasty, and Luka, Dog and Bear all ate very well and too quickly. However, they were aware that all the Rats in the place were watching them closely, staring with particular hostility at Bear the dog and Dog the bear, and that was an uneasy feeling. There was a lot of muttering at the other tables in what Luka thought must be Rattish, and then, finally, one particular Rat, a narrow-eyed, suspicious creature wearing a grey kepi, got up on its hind legs and walked over. He had clearly been chosen by his friends as the newcomers' interrogator. 'Ssso, ssstrangers,' said the Inquisitor Rat without preamble, 'may I asssk what you think of our great Resssspectorate of I?'

'I, I, sir, I, I, sir,' all the Rats in the Restau-Rat chorused.

'We love our country,' the Inquisitor Rat said coldly. 'And you? Do you love our country, too?'

'It's very nice,' Luka said carefully, 'and the food is excellent.'

The Inquisitor scratched his chin. 'Why am I not entirely convinced?' he asked, as if talking to himself. 'Why do I suspect there may be something insulting lurking beneath your superficial charm?'

'We must be going,' Luka said hastily, standing up. 'It was good to meet –' But the Inquisitor extended a claw-tipped arm and grasped Luka by the shoulder. 'Tell me this,' he demanded roughly. 'Do you believe that two and two make five?'

Luka hesitated, unsure of how to answer – whereupon, to his immense surprise, the Inquisitor leapt up onto the dining table, scattering plates and glasses in all directions, and burst into loud, hissy, tuneless song:

'Do you believe two and two make five?
Do you agree the world is flat?
Do you know our Bossss is the Biggest Cheese alive?
Do you Ressspect the Rat?
O, do you Ressspect the Rat?

If I sssay upside down is the right way round,
If I insissst that black is white,
If I claim that a sssqueak is the sssweetest sssound,
Do you ressspect my Right?
Say, do you Ressspect my Right?

Do you agree nothing's better than I?
Do you approve of my hat?
Will you please ssstop asking what, how and why?
Do you Ressspect the Rat?
Do you, don't you, don't you, do you,
. Do you Ressspect the Rat?'

And now all the Rats in the Restau-Rat leapt up on their
hind legs, placed their claws upon their chests, and sang the
chorus:

'I, I, sir,
I, I, sir,
We all say I, I, I.
There's no need to argue, no need to sussspect,
No need to think when you've got Ressspect,
We all say I, I, I.'

'That's just nonsense!' The words burst out of Luka before he could stop them. The Rats froze in their various poses, and then slowly, slowly, all their heads turned to look at Luka, and all their eyes glittered, and all their teeth were bared. 'This isn't good,' Luka thought, and Bear and Dog drew close to him, prepared to fight for their lives. Even Nobodaddy seemed, for once, nonplussed. The Rats faced Luka, and slowly, little Rat-step by little Rat-step, they closed in around him.

'Nonsenssse, you say,' mused the Inquisitor Rat. 'But, as it happens, it is also our National Sssong. Would you say, my fellow rodentsss, that this young rascal's Manners have been Minded? Or does he deserve – hmmm – a Black Mark?'

'Black Mark!' the Rats screeched, all together, and bared their terrible claws. And perhaps the story of Luka Khalifa's quest for the Fire of Life would have ended then and there at Alice's Restau-Rat, and maybe Dog the bear and Bear the dog would have been lost, too, though they would certainly have gone down fighting and taken many Rats with them; and then Nobodaddy would have returned to Kahani to wait until the life of Rashid Khalifa had filled him up completely . . . and how sad all of that would have been! Instead, however, there was a cry from the street outside, and enormous quantities of red gloop and what looked like gigantic amounts of egg yolk and, following that, a hail of rotten vegetables began to descend from the sky, and all the Rats forgot entirely about Luka and his cry of 'Nonsense!' and charged out into the street yelling, 'It's the Otters!' and, more simply, 'It's her again!' because the Respectorate of I was under attack from above, and leading her aerial squadrons in the attack, swooping high and low and left and right, standing upright and unafraid on her famous flying carpet, *Resham*, which is to say, the Green Silk Flying Rug of King Solomon the Wise, was the feared, the fabled, the ferocious, the fabulous Insultana of Ott, shouting out, through a powerful megaphone, her blood-curdling battlecry: '*We expectorate on the Respectorate!*'

'What's going on?' Luka shouted to Nobodaddy over the rising din, as the four travellers fled the Restau-Rat, just in case the Rats whom they had offended returned to finish them off. Outside in the street all was commotion and confusion and red gloop and egg and vegetables raining from above. They took shelter under the awning of a bakery down the road, its windows full of stale bread and unappetising-looking buns covered in grey icing. 'Over in that direction, Over The Top of those mountains,' Nobodaddy shouted back, pointing to a snow-capped range on the northern horizon, 'is the unusual land of Oh-Tee-Tee, a land ringed by bright waters, whose denizens, the Otters, are devoted to all forms of excess. They talk too much, eat too much, drink too much, sleep too much, swim too much, chew too much betel nut, and they are without any question the rudest creatures in the world. But it's an equal-opportunity impoliteness; the Otters all lay into one another without discrimination, and as a result they have all grown so thick-skinned that nobody minds what anyone else says. It's a funny place, everyone laughs all the time while they call one another the worst things in the world. That lady up there is the Sultana, their Queen, but because she's the most brilliant and sharp-tongued abuser of them all, everyone calls her the "Insult-ana". It was her idea to take the battle to the Respectorate, because she respects nobody and nothing. You could almost call Ott the "Disrespectorate", and dissing is unquestionably what they do best – Look at her!' he broke off, admiring the Queen. 'Isn't she gorgeous when she's angry?'

Luka looked up through the cascade of gloop, egg and vegetables. The Otter Queen was not an animal, but a green-eyed girl wearing a green-and-gold cloak, her fiery red hair streaming in the wind, no more than sixteen or seventeen years old. 'She's so young,' Luka said in surprise. Nobodaddy grinned Rashid Khalifa's grin. 'Young people can dish it out and take it better than old folks,' he said. 'They can forgive and forget. People my age . . . well, sometimes they bear grudges.' Luka frowned. 'Your age?' he said. 'But I thought . . .' Nobodaddy looked agitated. 'Your father's age, I meant. His age, obviously. Just a slip of the tongue.' This scared Luka a good deal. He noticed that Nobodaddy had almost stopped being transparent. Time was in shorter supply than he had hoped.

'We expectorate on the Respectorate!' the Insultana yelled again, and her yell unleashed even more of the red rain. Perhaps fifty other flying carpets were arrayed in battle formation around the Insultana above the streets of the Respectorate, all flapping gently in the breeze, and on each of them stood a tall, sleek, betel-nut-chewing Otter, spitting long, livid jets of red betel juice down upon the Respectorate, covering grey houses, grey streets and the grey populace with splashes of scarlet contempt. Rotten eggs, too, were being hurled by the Otters in enormous quantities, and the stink of sulphur dioxide filled the air. And after the rotten eggs, the decomposing veggies. It really was quite an assault, but what hurt most of all was the version of the 'National Song of I' that poured down on the Respectorate through the Insultana's megaphone. The Insultana sang in a high, clear voice – a voice that Luka thought oddly familiar, though he couldn't, for the moment, understand why.

'Two and two make four, not five.
The world is round, not flat.
Your Boss is the Smallest Fry alive.
We do not Respect the Rat!
O, we do not Respect the Rat!'

Splat! Baf! Whack! It was getting to be a terrible, messy scene. The battered Rats in the streets jumped in the air and flailed their claws uselessly above their heads, but the Insultana and her cohorts were far above them, out of reach.

'And upside down is the wrong way round,
And black is black, not white,
And a squeak is by far the creepiest of sounds,
No, we do not respect your Right,
We do not respect your Right.'

'We've got to get away!' shouted Luka, and ran out into the street. But the Border Post beyond which the *Argo* was moored was some little distance down the street, and before Luka had gone ten yards he was covered in betel juice and rotten eggs, and a rotten tomato had landed on his head. He noticed, too, that with each aerial strike the life-counter in the top left-hand corner of his field of vision went down by one. He was just deciding to make a run for it anyway when Nobodaddy grabbed him by the collar and dragged him back under the awning. 'Silly boy,' he said, not unkindly. 'Brave, but silly. That idea isn't going to fly. And besides, now that you've chosen the most difficult route, don't you want to save your progress?'

'Where's the saving point?' Luka asked, wiping the muck from his eyes and trying to get the tomato out of his hair. Nobodaddy pointed. 'There,' he said. Luka looked in the direction of Nobodaddy's pointing finger, and saw, arriving at the double, a phalanx of the largest and most ferocious rodents he had ever seen, armed to the teeth and firing their Ratapults furiously into the sky. These were the Respecto-Rats, of course, the most feared of the Respectorate's troops, and at their rear – 'leading from behind, that shows you what kind of a Rat he is,' Luka thought – was the Over-Rat himself, the one who looked exactly like . . . 'well, never mind that now,' Luka told himself. And some distance behind this advancing army stood the grey Rathouse, and at the apex of its grey dome, glistening in the sun, the one golden object in this world of grey, was a little Orb. 'That's it?' Luka cried. 'That's it all the way up there? How am I ever going to get to it?'

'I didn't say it would be easy,' Nobodaddy replied. 'But you still have nine hundred and nine lives left.'

Up in the sky the Otters on their flying carpets were dodging the Respecto-Rats' missiles with contemptuous ease, and they all sang together as they flew left and right and high and low, and swaying from side to side:

'Ai-yi,
Ai-yi,
We all moan ai-yi-yi.
You're fools and you're bullies,
Your thinking is woolly.
Respect? You're not serious?
Your effect's deleterious!
We laugh at you, ai-yi-yi-yi-yi,
We laugh at you, ai-yi-yi.'

'All right then,' said Luka, 'I'm tired of this place. If that's the button I have to push up there, then I'd better get up there now.' And without waiting for an answer, he began to run as fast as he could through the war-torn streets.

Even with Bear and Dog running interference for him, the task proved to be almost impossible. The assault of the Otters had reached a sort of climax, and Luka's losses of lives were alarming. Dodging the Respecto-Rats was tough, too, even though they weren't really thinking about him; their armoured gun carriers and motorbikes kept mowing him down as he ran. The Over-Rat, it became plain, was the only Rat who was watching out for Luka, as if he had some personal reason for being interested in the traveller's progress; and on those rare occasions when Luka managed to dodge the life-eating rain from the sky and avoid the Respecto-Rat forces, the Over-Rat zapped him without fail. And each time he was run over by an armoured car or bombed from the sky or zapped by the Over-Rat, whom he couldn't help picturing as Ratshit from school stuck in a really Ratty body, he lost a life and found himself back at his starting point, so he was getting nowhere fast, he was losing lives by the bushel, and being completely covered in rotten eggs and tomatoes and betel juice while he did so. After a long, long, frustrating time, he rested under the baker's shop awning, panting, soaked, smelly and with only 616 lives left, and complained to Nobodaddy, 'This is too hard. And why are those Otters so aggressive, anyway? Why can't they just live and let live?'

'Maybe they would,' Nobodaddy replied, 'if the Respectorate wasn't growing so fast. Those scary Respecto-Rats roam far beyond their own borders trying to force everyone into line. If things continue as they are, the whole World of Magic is in danger of being strangled by an excess of respect.'

'That's as may be,' Luka gasped, 'but when you're on the receiving end of the attack, it's hard to be sympathetic, to be honest with you. And look at the condition of my dog and my bear. I don't think they like Otters very much right now, either.'

'Sometimes,' Nobodaddy reflected, almost as though he were talking to himself, 'the solution is to run towards the problem, not away from it.'

'I am trying to run towards –' began Luka, and then he stopped. 'Oh,' he said. 'I see what you're saying. Not the golden ball. That's not the problem, is it?'

'Not at present,' Nobodaddy agreed.

Luka squinted up into the sky. There she was, the Insultana, the Fairy Queen of the Otters, monarch of the skies, riding on King Solomon's Carpet. She looked sixteen or seventeen but she was probably really thousands of years old, he thought, the way magical creatures were. 'What's her name?' he wondered.

Nobodaddy looked pleased in the way that Rashid Khalifa looked pleased when Luka did well at mathematical calculation. 'Exactly,' he said. 'Knowing a magic creature's name gives you power over it, yes it does! If you knew her name you could call her and she would have to come. Unfortunately, she is known by dozens of names, and maybe none of them are the real one. Keep your own name secret, that's my advice. Because if they know your name in the Magic World, who knows what they might do with it.'

'Do you know her name, then,' Luka said impatiently, 'or are you going on and on in this way to hide the fact that you don't?'

'Ooh, that stings,' said Nobodaddy languidly, fanning himself with his hat. 'What a sharp little tongue! You'd make a good Otter. As a matter of fact,' he went on hastily, seeing Luka open his mouth again, 'I've narrowed it down. After much thought and analysis, I've got it down to half a dozen. Six of the best. I'm pretty sure it's one of those.'

'"Pretty sure" isn't very impressive,' Luka said.

'I haven't had a chance to try them out,' Nobodaddy replied, sounding indignant. 'But why don't you have a go right now and we'll settle the matter once and for all?'

So Luka called out the names Nobodaddy gave him, one by one. 'Bilqis! Makeda! Saba! Kandaka! Nicaula!' The woman on the flying carpet ignored them all. Nobodaddy, looking crestfallen, suggested a few more names, but with decreasing conviction. Luka tried them too. 'Meroë! Nana! Um . . . *what* did you say?'

'Chalchiuhtlicue,' Nobodaddy repeated doubtfully.

'Chalchi . . .' Luka began, then stopped.

'. . . uhtlicue,' Nobodaddy prompted.

'Chalchiuhtlicue,' Luka shouted, triumphantly.

'It means "the woman in the jade skirt",' Nobodaddy explained.

'I don't care what it means,' said Luka, 'because it's having no effect, so it obviously isn't her name.'

For a moment Luka fell into a terrible sadness. He would never be able to get out of this mess, never be able to find the Fire of Life or save his father. This strange version of his father, Nobodaddy, was the only father he had now, and he wouldn't have him for long, either. He would lose his father and his father's fatal copy; it was time to get used to that horrible fact. All he would have left was his mother, and her beautiful voice . . .

'I know the Insultana's name,' he said suddenly, and stepping out from the shadow of the awning, he called in a loud, clear voice, 'Soraya!'

Time stopped. The descending jets of betel juice, the rotten tomatoes, the egg missiles froze in mid-flight; the Rats became motionless, like photographs of themselves; in the sky the Otters stood still on their carpets in attitudes of war, and the flying rugs, as if turned to stone, no longer flapped in the breeze; even Bear, Dog and Nobodaddy were as stiff as waxworks. In all that timeless universe only two people moved. One was Luka; the other, swooping down on King Solomon's Carpet, *Resham*, and coming to a halt right in front of him, was the brilliant and slightly frightening Insultana of Ott. Except that Luka wasn't scared of her. This was his father's World of Magic, and therefore it was to be expected that this young Queen, the most important female person in that world, had the same name as Luka's mother, the most important woman in his, and his father's, world. 'You summoned me,' she said. 'You guessed my name, which stopped Time, so here I am. What do you want?'

There are moments in life – not enough of them, but they do occur – when even young boys find exactly the right words to say at exactly the right time; when, like a gift, the right idea occurs to you just when you most need it. This, for Luka, was one such moment. He found himself saying to the great ruler of Ott, without fully knowing where in his head he had found the words, 'I believe we can help each other, Insultana Soraya. There is something I need you to help me with, urgently, and in return I have an idea for you that might just win you this war.'

Soraya leaned forward. 'Just tell me what you want from me,' she commanded, in her rough Otter way, and Luka, his usually fluent tongue paralysed, pointed to the golden ball atop the Rathouse dome. 'Yes, I see,' said Soraya of Ott, 'and afterwards, my young milord, no doubt you will wish to return to the River and be on your way.' Luka nodded dumbly, not even surprised by how much the Insultana knew. 'That is nothing,' she said, and motioned Luka to come aboard the flying carpet, revealing a kinder nature than her sharp words implied.

An instant later the carpet took off, with Luka, caught off balance, lying flat on his back upon it; and an instant after that, they were at the golden ball, and Luka was able to get up and thump it, and heard the satisfying *ding* of a level being saved, and saw in the upper right-hand corner of his field of vision the single-digit number climbing to 2. And then they were down on the ground again, next to Nobodaddy and Dog and Bear, all of whom were still frozen in time, and Soraya was saying, 'Now it's your turn. Or was that just big talk? Boys like you – you're all mouth and no trousers, as the saying goes.'

'Itching powder,' Luka said humbly, thinking that it didn't sound like such an impressive idea. But the Insultana was listening hard now, so Luka went ahead and told her, shyly and with considerable embarrassment, about his own military history, and the victory over the Imperial Highness Army in the Great Playground Wars. Soraya gave the impression of hanging on his every word, and when he had finished she gave a low, impressed whistle.

'Itching-powder bombs,' she said, mostly to herself. 'Why did we never think of that? Those could work. Rats hate itches! Those should work. Yes! They *will* work!' To Luka's amazement and secret delight, she leaned down and kissed him three times, on the left cheek, then the right, and then the left again. 'Thank you,' she said. 'You are a man of your word.'

It was said of the Flying Carpet of King Solomon that it could carry any number of people, no matter how large that number might be, and any weight of goods, no matter how heavy that weight, and that it could grow until it was immensely large, as much as sixty miles long and sixty miles wide. When the weather called for shade, an army of birds would gather above it like a parasol, and the wind would blow it wherever it wanted to go, as fast as the blinking of an eye. But these were only stories, and what Luka saw next he saw with his own eyes: the Insultana

Soraya spread her arms wide, and the wind leapt up at her bidding. Then she quite simply disappeared, and, no more than ninety seconds later, reappeared; but this time the carpet was much larger and on it were literally tens of thousands of small paper airplanes. It was obvious that the ruler of Ott was capable of getting things done pretty quickly. An instant after her reappearance, the paper airplanes had taken flight and distributed themselves among all the members of her personal air force, which was still frozen in time like everything else as far as Luka could see. In the whole observable world only he and the Insultana and the armada of paper planes were moving. Also the green-and-gold Carpet of King Solomon, which, after passing out its cargo, returned to the size of a largish domestic rug.

'How did you do that?' Luka asked, and then added, 'Never mind,' knowing the answer before it was given. 'I know. A P2C2E, and the itching-powder bombs were made at super-speed by M2C2Ds. Machines Too Complicated To Describe.'

'I'm willing to bet,' said the Insultana, 'that you didn't learn that at school.'

Many things make rats feel like scratching themselves, and there is nothing as unhappy as an itchy rodent. Rats get parasites – lice and mites and fleas – and these tiny bugs lay eggs at the base of the rats' hairs, and they itch. Rats lead rough lives in dirty places and they get cuts and the cuts get infected and become sores and then the sores itch. Rats' hair falls out and that makes their skin itch. Their skin gets dry, and they suffer from dandruff, and that's itchy as well. Rats eat all kinds of garbage and so they suffer from food allergies and eating too much of one thing and not enough of another and all that makes them itch like crazy. Rats suffer from eczema and ring-worm and they get scabs and rashes and they can't resist scratching them, even if the scratching makes things worse. And whatever could be said of rats in general was magnified in the case of the giant Rats of the Respectorate, the famously thin-skinned Rats of I. And however itchy the Respectorate rodents might have been in the past, they had never experienced anything like the itchiness that was unleashed upon them by the Otter Queen and her air force.

'Before I unfreeze everyone,' the Insultana instructed Luka, 'take your friends indoors and wait until I tell you it's safe to come out.' Her tone had changed completely, Luka noted; no trace of sharpness remained. In fact, it was positively friendly, even affectionate.

Luka did as the Insultana told him, hustling his little party into the grey bakery and then pressing up against the glass windowpane; so he and Dog and Bear and Nobodaddy only saw a little bit of the large-scale destruction that followed. The Insultana waved an imperious arm and the Respectorate unfroze. Now Luka watched the Otters swooping and diving around the city streets unleashing their enchanted paper planes, which seemed to be equipped with Rat-seeking homing devices and chased the Rats wherever they went, indoors and outdoors, under their bed sheets or up on roofs, and it wasn't long before the attack succeeded and had the Rats on the run. Betel juice and eggs and rotten vegetables had been effective as insults, but the itching powder didn't just hurt the Rats' feelings and ruin their clothes and make them smell even worse than they did already. Luka saw even the nastiest-looking giant Rats – the mirror-shade-wearing, heavily armed, super-nasty Respecto-Rats of I – running in circles and screaming as the paper planes chased them and poured itching powder on their heads and down the backs of their necks. He saw them tearing at themselves with their long angry claws and ripping great lumps off their own bodies as they tried to stop the itching. The air was full of Rat shrieks, growing louder and louder, so loud that Luka had to cover his ears because it was almost too much to bear.

'If that powder is what I think it is,' Nobodaddy said at last, in a voice filled with wonder, 'if that is indeed made, as I believe it may be, from the deadly Asian Khujli plant, mixed up, I don't doubt, with powder from the seeds of Alifbay's own, over-powering, though rare, Gudgudi flower . . . and if the Insultana has included material from the Sickening Yuckbone or Magic Itch Bean of Germany, spores from the Demonic Abraxas of Egypt, the Kachukachu of Peru, and whirligigs from Africa's Fatal Pipipi, then we may be witnessing the end of the Rat Infestation of the Magical World. What is interesting about the formula which I believe the Insultana may have used is that ordinary people are immune to these occult powders; rodents alone are affected. Yes, she asked you to take shelter, but that was to protect the dog and the bear, as a precautionary measure; and above all, I surmise, to save us all from the Rats possessed of their last and lethal Frenzy.'

The Rats had indeed taken leave of their senses. Through the window of the grey bakery, Luka witnessed their mounting insanity and their dying throes. The thin-skinned masters of the Respectorate were literally scratching themselves to bits, actually ripping themselves apart, until there was nothing left of them but lumps of mangy fur and grey, ugly meat. The shrieking of the Rats reached a terrible crescendo, and then slowly the air grew quieter, and silence fell. At the very end Luka saw the Over-Rat himself come running down the street towards the River of Time, slashing himself as he ran, and at the end of the street he leapt into the River with a terrible cry and, as he was the one Rat in the World of Magic who was unable to swim, because he had always been too lazy and spoiled to take the trouble to learn, he drowned in the Temporal Flow.

And that was the end of that.

Slowly, slowly, the non-Rat inhabitants of the Respectorate came out of their homes and understood that their ordeal was at an end, and then in great happiness they rushed to the fences that separated the Respectorate from the rest of the Magical World and tore them down and flung away the broken remnants of their prison walls for ever. And if any Rats did survive the Great Itch Bombing they were never seen again, but crawled back into the darkness behind the cracks of the world, which was where Rats belonged.

Soraya of Ott on her green-and-gold carpet landed outside the grey bakery as Luka and his companions emerged. 'Luka Khalifa,' she said, and Luka didn't even ask her how she knew his name, 'you have done the World of Magic a great service. Aren't you going to ask me for anything else in return? You guessed my name; that alone should get you at least the traditional three wishes, and you've only used up one. But for the idea of the Itch Bombs! Who knows what's a fair reward for that. Why don't you just think of the biggest, most important wish you can come up with, and I'll see if I can do anything to help?'

And before Nobodaddy could stop him, Luka began to talk very fast, to tell this astonishing young girl who had the same name as his mother exactly why he was here in the World of Magic, and what he hoped to do, and why. By the end of his little speech the Sultana of Ott's eyes had widened and her hand had risen to her mouth. 'Perhaps, in my pride, I spoke too soon,' she said, and there was a note of awe in her voice. 'It may be that you have asked me for a thing I cannot give.'

But then she grinned a mischievous grin and clapped her hands like a child. 'To steal the Fire of Life, which has never been done in the whole history of the Magical World! Why, that would be the most deliciously Disrespectful Deed in All of Time! It would be outrageous, and wonderful. In a phrase, it would be completely Over The Top, and therefore it behoves any true Otter to help. My fellow warriors of the OAF, the Otter Air Force, must return home to Ott – but, Luka Khalifa, Thief of Fire, I, the Queen of the Otters, will do everything in my power to assist you to perpetrate your dreadful – and most noble, and most dangerous, and absolutely most enjoyable! – Crime.'

'I'm in a sort of hurry,' said Luka bravely, 'and you have this super fast carpet. Is there any way you could rush me past all the other levels and take me right to the Fire, where I need to be, and afterwards get me back where I started from?'

'The River is long and deceptive,' said Insultana Soraya,

nodding thoughtfully. 'And you still have to pass through the Mists of Time, where you can't see a thing, and then there's the Great Stagnation, where the River turns into a swamp and you can't move, and the Inescapable Whirlpool, where Time spins round and round and you can't escape, and the Trillion and One Forking Paths, where the River becomes a labyrinth – and you will certainly get lost in all those mazy waterways and never find the one single stream that is the true, continuous Path of Time. Very well,' she said, in a voice that told Luka that a decision had been made, 'I will join you in your adventure. There are at least those four stages – what did you call them? – "levels"? – four levels that I can enable you to skip. But after that we will just have to take things as they come.'

'Why can't you take me all the way?' Luka blurted out, very disappointed.

'Because, my sweet Luka,' replied the Insultana of Ott, 'this silken flying carpet given to me so long ago by King Solomon himself can do many wondrous things, but it cannot fly through the Great Rings of Fire.'

5

The Path to the Three Fiery Doughnuts

If you have not yet flown on a magic carpet, you probably don't
know about the seasickness. A flying carpet makes a slow, rolling,
wavelike movement as it passes through the air, not exactly as
if it's floating on airwaves, but more as if the carpet itself has
become a kind of silken air that can bear you aloft and take you
wherever you want to go. It's sad, but true, that your stomach
may find this kind of travel disagreeable, at least for a while. And
if you have never flown on a flying carpet accompanied by a
nervous talking bear, an even more nervous talking dog, and an
Elephant Duck and an Elephant Drake making the first flight of
their otherwise flightless lives, to say nothing of a supernatural
being who looks, acts and talks like your own father, as well as
an ancient Queen who looks, acts and talks like a seventeen-
year-old girl, and, in addition, a large amphibian boat tank named
Argo, then you will just have to imagine the confusion that
reigned aboard the green-and-gold *Resham* as it took off to begin
its journey towards the Mists of Time. The flying carpet had
grown considerably in size to accommodate all its passengers
and cargo, and this exaggerated the waviness of the flight.

It was, it has to be said, a chaotic and noisy scene. There was a moaning and a howling and a groaning and a growling, and that honking sound elephants (and ducks) make when they are in distress. Dog the bear kept saying that if bears had been meant to fly they would have grown wings, and he mentioned, too, that when bears sat on carpets it made them think of bearskin rugs, but mainly it was the flying thing that was the problem; and Bear the dog was babbling anxiously and without stopping as he rolled around the rug, and his monologue went something like this: *I'm going to fall off, aren't I? I am, don't let me fall, am I going to fall off? I am, I can tell, I'm going to fall off, any second now, I'll fall*; even though in fact the carpet carefully curved itself upwards whenever any of the travellers lurched too close to an edge, and deposited them safely back at, or near, the centre.

As for the Elephant Birds, they kept asking each other why they were there at all. In the excitement of the departure from the Respectorate, they had somehow been swept aboard along with the *Argo*, but they couldn't remember being asked if they would actually like to come. 'And if we can't remember it, it didn't happen,' said the Elephant Drake. They felt kidnapped, shanghaied, dragged along on an adventure that had nothing to do with them and was very probably extremely dangerous, and yes, they thought they might fall off the rug as well.

Of course the Insultana Soraya abused the lot of them roundly, as it was in her nature to do, calling them babies and girls and boobies and not-ducks-but-geese; she told them they were scaredy-cats and namby-pambies, sissies and yellow-bellies, milksops and Milquetoasts and candy-asses (a term with which Luka was not familiar, though he thought he could probably work out what it meant). She made chicken noises at them to call them cowards, and the worst part of all was when she squeaked at them contemptuously, which meant she was calling them mice.

Nobodaddy, naturally, handled the flying-carpet ride effortlessly, and stood coolly and with perfect assurance beside the Insultana, and that made Luka determined to find his 'carpet legs' as soon as possible. After a while he did, and stopped falling over; and after a further while the four animals found their twelve legs as well, and then, at last, the moaning and groaning stopped and things settled down, and nobody had actually been sick.

Once he could stand up and keep his balance on the flying carpet, Luka noticed that he was getting extremely cold. The carpet was beginning to fly higher and faster, and his teeth were beginning to chatter. The Insultana Soraya did not seem to be affected by the cold, even though she was wearing floaty garments that appeared to be constructed out of cobwebs and butterflies' wings, and neither did Nobodaddy, who stood beside her in Rashid Khalifa's short-sleeved vermilion bush shirt, looking quite unconcerned. Dog the bear seemed fine under all that hair, and the Elephant Drake and Duck had their downy feathers to keep them warm, but Bear the dog looked shivery and Luka was getting very cold indeed. 'Who would have thought,' Luka mused, 'that this business of flying through the air would present so many practical problems?' Inevitably the Insultana called him a whole set of new names when she saw that he was freezing to death. 'I suppose,' she said, 'that you expected this flying carpet to have central heating and whatnot. But this, my dear, is no modern softie's suburban deep-shag-pile rug. This, I'll have you know, is an *antique*.'

When Soraya had finished teasing Luka, however, she clapped her hands, and at once an old oak chest – which Luka had not noticed until that moment, but which had apparently been aboard the flying carpet the whole time – sprang open, and out flew two seemingly flimsy shawls. One shawl flew into Luka's hands and the other wrapped itself around Bear. When Luka put the shawl around him he immediately began to feel as if he had been transported to somewhere in the tropics – almost too warm, almost as if he would prefer it to be a little cooler. 'Some people are never satisfied,' said the Insultana, reading his mind, and she turned away from him to hide her affectionate grin.

Now that he was warm as well as balanced, Luka was able to take in the wonderful sight that lay before him. The flying carpet was following the course of the River of Time. The World of Magic lay spread out on both banks of the River, and Luka, the storyteller's son, began to recognise all the places he knew so well from his father's tales. The landscape was dotted with cities, and with a rising excitement and a pounding heart Luka recognised them all, Khwáb, the City of Dreams, and Umeed Nagar, the City of Hope, and Zamurrad, the Emerald City, and Baadal-Garh, the Fortress City built upon a Cloud. In the distance to the east, rising up against the horizon, were the blue hills of the Land of Lost Childhood, and in the west lay the Undiscovered Country, and there – over there – was the Place Where Nobody Lived. Luka recognised with a thrill the crazy architecture of the House of Games and the Hall of Mirrors, and beside them the gardens of Paradise, Gulistan and Bostan, and, most exciting of all, the large Country of Imaginary Beings, Peristan, in which the peris, or fairies, endlessly did battle with malevolent ogres known as *devs* or *bhoots*. 'I wish I wasn't in such a hurry,' Luka thought, because this was the world he had always thought of as being even better than his own, the world he had drawn and painted all his life.

He also saw, now that he was aloft and could take it all in, the enormous size of the Magic World, and the colossal length of the River of Time; and he understood that he would never have been able to get where he needed to go if he had had to rely on the Memory of the Elephant Birds for fuel, and their pulling power for speed. But now the Flying Carpet of King Solomon was carrying him at a great rate towards his goal, and even though he knew there would be dangers ahead he entered a state of high excitement, because, thanks to the Insultana of Ott, the impossible had just become a little more possible. And then he saw the Mists of Time.

At first they were no more than a white, cloudy mass on the horizon, but their true immensity became apparent as the carpet hurtled towards them. They stretched from horizon to horizon like a soft wall across the world, flowing across the River's course and swallowing it up, engulfing the enchanted landscape and gobbling the sky. Any moment now they would fill Luka's entire field of vision, and then there would be no Magic World left, only these clammy Mists. Luka felt the optimism and excitement drain out of him and a cold, bad feeling crept into the pit of his stomach. He felt Soraya's hand on his shoulder, but did not feel reassured.

'We have reached the Limits of Memory,' Nobodaddy announced. 'This is as far as your hybrid, surf-and-turf friends here would have been able to bring you.' The Elephant Birds were most displeased. 'We are not accustomed,' said the Elephant Duck with immense dignity, 'to being described as menu items.' (That had been the true Nobodaddy speaking, Luka realised, the creature he didn't like, and indeed had every reason not to like. His own father would never have said such a thing.) 'Also,' said the Elephant Drake, 'may we remind you of the old cautionary saying regarding what you should do when you reach the Limits of even an elephantine Memory?'

'What should you do?' Luka asked.

'Duck,' said the Elephant Duck.

No sooner had she spoken than a fusillade of missiles came flying out of the Mists of Time, and the carpet had to take swift evasive action, diving and climbing and swerving to right and left. (The animals and Luka lost their balance again, and once more there was much rolling about and many noisy ursine, canine and duck-elephantine protests.) The missiles seemed to be made out of the same substance as the Mists themselves: they were white Mistballs the size of large cannonballs. 'Can they really hurt us that much if they're made out of fog?' Luka asked. 'What happens if one of them hits you?' Nobodaddy shook his head. 'Don't underestimate the Weapons of Time,' he said. 'If a Mistball struck you, your entire memory would immediately be erased. You would not remember your life, or your language, or even who you were. You would become an empty shell, good for nothing, finished.' That silenced Luka. If that was what a Mistball could do, he was thinking, what would happen when they plunged into the Mists of Time themselves? They wouldn't stand a chance. He must have been crazy to think he could penetrate all the defences of the Magic World and reach the Heart of Time itself. He was just a boy, and the job he had given himself was far beyond his capabilities. If he went on, it would mean not only his own destruction but the ruin of his friends. He couldn't do it; but, on the other hand, he couldn't stop, because to stop would be to give up hope for his father, however slim that hope might be.

'Don't worry so much,' Soraya of Ott said, interrupting his anguished thoughts. 'You are not defenceless here. Have some faith in the great Flying Carpet of King Solomon the Wise.'

Luka's spirits lifted a little, but only a little. 'Does somebody know we are coming?' he wondered. 'Mustn't that be why the missiles were fired?'

'Not necessarily,' said Nobodaddy. 'I believe we may have triggered an automatic defence system by coming so close to the Mists of Time. We are about to break the Rules of History, after all, young Luka. When we enter the Mists we will leave behind the world of Living Memory and move towards Eternity; that is,' he went on, seeing from the confusion on Luka's face that he needed to be clearer, 'towards the secret zone, where clocks do not tick, and Time stands still. Not one of us is supposed to be there. Let me put it like this. When a bug of some sort enters your system, when it starts moving around your body and making you feel unwell, your body dispatches Antibodies to fight it until it's destroyed, and you start feeling better. In this case, I'm afraid, we are the bugs, and so we must expect . . . opposition.'

When Luka was just six years old he had seen pictures of the planet Jupiter on television, pictures beamed back to Earth by a tiny, unmanned space probe that was actually falling slowly towards the surface of that great gas giant of a planet. Every day the probe got closer and the planet loomed larger and larger. The pictures clearly showed the slow movement of the gases of Jupiter, the way they created layers of colour and movement, arranging themselves in stripes and swirls, and, of course, forming the two famous Spots, the huge one and the smaller one. In the end the probe was pulled down by the planet's gravitational force and disappeared for ever, with what Luka imagined to be a soft *gloop*, a slow sucking sound, and after that there were no more pictures of Jupiter on television. As the flying carpet *Resham* approached the Mists of Time, Luka could see that their surface, too, was full of movement, just like Jupiter's. The Mists, too, flowed and swirled and were full of intricate patterns, and there were colours there, too – as Luka got closer and closer he could see the whiteness breaking up into many subtly graded hues. 'We are the probe,' he thought, 'a manned probe, not an unmanned one, but any second now there will probably be a *gloop*, and that will be that. End of transmission.'

The Mists were upon him, all-encompassing and blinding, and then, with no sort of a sound at all, the flying carpet had entered the whiteness, but the Mists of Time touched none of them, because the carpet, too, possessed defence mechanisms, and had put up some sort of invisible shield around itself, a force field that was plainly strong enough to keep the Mists at bay. Safe in this little bubble, just as Soraya had promised they would be – *have faith in the carpet*, she had said – the travellers began the Crossing.

'Oh, goodness,' cried the Elephant Duck, 'we are going into Oblivion. What an awful thing to ask a Memory Bird to do.'

★   ★   ★

It was like being blind, Luka thought, except maybe blindness was full of colours and shapes, of brightnesses and darknesses and dots and flashes, which, after all, was how things looked behind his eyelids whenever he closed his eyes. He knew that deafness could fill up your ears with static and all sorts of buzzing, ringing sounds, so perhaps blindness filled up your eyes in the same useless way. This blindness was different, though; it felt, well, *absolute*. He remembered Nobodaddy asking him, 'What was there before the Bang?' and realised that this whiteness, this absence of everything, might be the answer. You couldn't even call it a place. It was what there was when there wasn't a place to be in. Now he knew what people meant when they talked about things being lost in the Mists of Time. When people said that it was just a figure of speech, but these Mists were not just words. They were what there was before there were any words at all.

The whiteness wasn't the same as blankness, though; it moved, it was active, stirring round and round the carpet, like a broth made out of nothing. Nothing Soup. The carpet was flying as fast as it could, and that was very, very fast, but it seemed to be motionless. In the bubble there was no wind, and around the bubble there was nothing to look at that might give you the feeling of movement. It would probably have felt the same, Luka thought, if the carpet had stopped dead in the middle of the Mists, so that they were marooned there for ever. And the moment he thought that, that was how it began to feel. They weren't moving at all. Here in this time before Time they were adrift, forgotten, lost. What was it the Elephant Duck had called this place? *Oblivion*. The place of total forgetting, of nothingness, of not-being. *Limbo*, religious people used to say. The place between Heaven and Hell.

Luka felt alone. He wasn't alone, obviously, everyone was still there, but he felt horribly lonely. He wanted his mother, he missed his brother, he wished his father hadn't fallen Asleep. He wanted his room, his friends, his street, his neighbourhood, his school. He wanted his life to go back to being the way it had always been. The Mists of Time curled around the carpet and he began to imagine fingers in the whiteness, long tendril-like fingers clutching at him, trying to grab him and wipe him clean. Alone in the Mists of Time (even though not actually alone) he began to wonder what on earth he had done. He had broken the first rule of childhood – *don't talk to strangers* – and had actually allowed a stranger to take him away from safety into the least safe place he had ever seen in his life. So he was a fool and would probably pay for his folly. And who was this stranger, anyway? He said he had not been *sent* but *summoned*. As if a dying man – and, yes, there in the Mists of Time Luka was at last able to say that word, if only to himself in the privacy of his thoughts – as if his dying father would summon his own death. He wasn't sure whether he believed that or not. How stupid was it to go off into the blue – into the white – with a person – a *creature*! – you didn't entirely believe or wholly trust? Luka had always been thought of as a sensible boy, but he had just disproved that theory, big time. He was the least sensible boy he knew.

He looked across at his dog and his bear. Neither of them spoke, but he could see in their eyes that they, too, were in the grip of a deep loneliness. The stories they had told when they acquired the power of speech, the stories of their lives, seemed to be slipping away from them. Perhaps they had never been those people, perhaps those were just dreams they had had, banal dreams of being noblemen; didn't everyone dream of being a prince? The truth of those stories slipped away from them, here in the white, white void, and they were just animals again, and going towards an uncertain doom.

Then at last there was a change. The whiteness thinned out. It was no longer everything and everywhere, but more like thick clouds in the sky as an airplane rushes through them, and there was something up ahead – yes! an opening – and here again was the forgotten sensation of speed, the feeling of the carpet going like a rocket towards the light, which was close now, and closer still, and finally *whoooossssshhhh* out they came into the light of a bright, sunny day. Everybody aboard the *Resham* was cheering loudly in their various fashions, and Luka, touching his cheeks, realised to his surprise that they were wet with tears. He heard a now-familiar *ding*, and the counter in the top right-hand corner of his field of vision climbed to 3. In all the excitement he hadn't even seen the saving point, so how? 'You weren't looking,' said Soraya. 'That's okay. I saved it for you.'

He looked down and saw the Great Stagnation. On this side of the Mists of Time, the River had expanded into a gigantic Swamp, which spread in every direction, as far as the eye could see. 'It looks beautiful,' he said. 'It is beautiful,' Soraya replied, 'if beauty is what you're looking for. Down there you'll find rare alligators and giant woodpeckers and scented cypress trees and carnivorous sundew plants. But you will also lose your way, and indeed yourself, for it is in the nature of the Great

Stagnation to capture all who stray into it by inducing a sleepy laziness, a desire to remain there for ever, to ignore your true purpose and your old life and simply lie down under a tree and rest. The perfumes of the Stagnation are exceptional, too, but they are by no means innocent. Breathe in that beauty and you'll smile contentedly and lie back on a tussock of grass . . . and be the captive of the Swamp for good.'

'Thank goodness for you and your flying carpet,' said Luka gratefully. 'Meeting you was the luckiest day of my life.'

'Or the unluckiest,' said Soraya of Ott. 'Because all I can do is bring you closer and closer to the greatest dangers you will ever face.'

That was a pleasant thought.

'Don't be tricked,' the Insultana added, 'by the golden Save button. There it is, right at the edge of the Stagnation, but if we go down there to punch it, we'll breathe that goodnight scent and fall asleep and that will be the end of us. It's not necessary, anyway. When we save at the end of the Forking Paths, it will automatically save the earlier levels.'

The idea of skipping the saving points made Luka nervous, because if for some reason he lost a life, would he have to cross the Great Stagnation all over again? 'Don't worry about that,' Soraya said. 'Worry about this instead.' She was pointing straight ahead. In the distance Luka could make out the rim of a low, flat cloud formation that looked like it was spinning slowly round and round. 'The Inescapable Whirlpool is under that,' said Soraya. 'Have you ever heard of El Niño?' Luka frowned. 'It's that warm spot in the ocean, right?' The Insultana of Ott looked impressed. 'The Pacific Ocean,' she said. 'It's enormous, as big as Amreeka, and it shows up every seven or eight years and plays havoc with the weather.' Luka knew that, or he remembered it when she said it, anyway. 'What does that have to do with us?' he asked. 'We're nowhere near the Pacific Ocean.' Soraya pointed again. 'That,' she said, 'is El Tiempo. It's also as big as Amreeka, it also shows up every seven or eight years, right above the Whirlpool, and when it does, it does terrible things to Time. If you fall into the Whirlpool, where Time spins round, you're stuck for ever, but if El Tiempo gets you, things start going a little crazy.'

'But we're too high up to be trapped by it, aren't we?' Luka anxiously asked.

'Let's hope so,' Queen Soraya replied. Then she called for everyone's attention. 'To avoid being caught up in the unpredictable temporal distortions of the El Tiempo phenomenon,' she announced, 'I will reduce the carpet to the smallest size that can carry us all, and the *Argo* also, of course, large as she is. I will also be taking the carpet to its maximum height and will reactivate the shields to keep you all warm and to make sure there is air to breathe.' This was serious. Everyone gathered at the centre of the rug and the edges closed in around them. The force field came on, and Soraya added, 'I should tell you that this is the last time I will be able to use the shield, or else it will not have enough power left to get us back again.' Luka wanted to ask her where the carpet's power source was and how it was recharged, but judging by the expression on her face this was not the right time for inquisitive questions. Her eyes stayed fixed on the approaching El Tiempo, with the Inescapable Whirlpool below. And now the carpet began to rise.

The Kármán Line, the edge of the Earth's atmosphere, is –

to put it simply – the line above which there isn't enough air to support a flying carpet. That is the true frontier of our world, beyond which lies outer space, and it's roughly sixty-two miles, or one hundred kilometres, above sea level. This was one of those useless facts that had become stuck in Luka's memory on account of his great interest in intergalactic fiction, video games and science-fiction movies, and, goodness, he thought, it turned out not to be so useless after all, because that appeared to be where they were going. Up and up went the *Resham*, and the sky turned black and the stars began to shine, and even though they were protected by the carpet's force field they all felt the chill of Infinity, and the bleak emptiness of space suddenly didn't seem exciting at all.

Far, far below them as they climbed – perhaps *forty miles* below them already – swirled the Inescapable Whirlpool, creating loops in Time, and above it the treacherous El Tiempo; but even though they were as far from danger as it was possible to be, they were still in double trouble, because far, far below them as they climbed – perhaps *forty miles* below them already – swirled the Inescapable Whirlpool, creating loops in Time, and above it the treacherous El Tiempo; but even though they were as far from danger as it was possible to be, they were still in double trouble, because far, far below them as they climbed – perhaps *forty miles* below them already – swirled the Inescapable Whirlpool, creating loops in Time, and above it the treacherous El Tiempo; but even though they were as far from danger as it was possible to be, they were still in double trouble, because far, far below them – perhaps *forty miles* below them already – swirled the Inescapable Whirlpool, creating loops in Time, and above it the treacherous El Tiempo; but even though they were as far from danger as it was possible to be, they were still in double trouble, because far, far below them as they climbed – and here the carpet broke out of the temporal whirlpool with a jerk that sent even Nobodaddy flying.

Only Soraya remained upright. 'That's one problem dealt with,' she said, but she didn't look seventeen any more, Luka realised, she looked maybe one hundred and seventeen, one thousand and seventeen years old, while he himself seemed to be getting younger by the minute, and Bear the dog was a puppy while Dog the bear looked rickety and frail. Even Nobodaddy had grown a white beard that reached down to his knees. If this went on much longer, Luka realised, they could forget about the Fire of Life, because El Tiempo would defeat them right here and now – whenever *now* was in this zone of messed-up years.

Once again, however, the Carpet of King Solomon proved equal to the task. Further and further it climbed, higher and higher, straining against the pull of the temporal traps below. And after a long, worrying time the moment came, the moment for which Luka had almost not dared to hope, when the *Resham* broke free of El Tiempo's dark, invisible bonds. 'We're free,' Soraya cried, and her face was her beautiful young face once again, and Bear was no longer a puppy, and Dog looked strong and fit. They were at the very zenith of their journey, just below the Kármán Line, and Luka stared with a kind of enchanted terror into the deeps of space, deciding that perhaps he preferred to keep his feet on the ground after all. And in a while the carpet began to descend, and El Tiempo and the Whirlpool were behind them. There had been no way to reach the saving point, wherever it might have been. So the risks were growing. If for any reason Luka failed to punch the golden button at the end of the next level he would be condemned to defeat this one all over again, and without the benefit of the carpet's shields he would not stand a chance. But there was no time for such defeatist thinking. The Trillion and One Forking Paths lay ahead.

They were approaching the upper reaches of the River of Time. The wide, lazy lower River was far behind them, and so was the treacherous middle. As they got closer to the River's source in the Lake of Wisdom, the River's flow should have dwindled, making it an ever narrower stream. And no doubt it had; but now there were numberless other streams all around it, streams flowing in and out of one another, looking from above like the myriad strands of an intricate, liquid tapestry. Which one was the River of Life? 'They all look the same to me,' Luka confessed. And Soraya had a confession of her own. 'This is the level I'm least certain about,' she said, a little shamefacedly. 'But don't worry! I'll get you there! That's an Otter promise!' Luka was horrified. 'You mean, when you said you could help me skip four levels, you weren't sure about the last one? And we haven't even saved our progress, so if you get this wrong we'll be done for, we'll have to do the last two all over again . . . ?' The Insultana was not accustomed to criticism, and her face coloured brightly; and she and Luka might have had quite a quarrel right then and there, if there hadn't been loud harrumphing noises to distract them. But harrumphing noises there were, and they turned crossly away from each other to see what was going on.

'Excuse me,' harrumphed the Elephant Duck, 'but aren't you ignoring something important?'

'Or some*one*,' said the Elephant Drake. 'Two someones, in fact.'

'Us,' the Elephant Duck clarified.

'Who are we?' the Elephant Drake wanted to know. 'Are we living-room ornaments, or are we, perhaps, the famous Memory Birds of the World of Magic?'

'Are we surf-and-turf menu items,' the Elephant Duck went on, with a glare in Nobodaddy's direction, 'or have we perhaps spent our whole lives swimming in the River of Time, fishing for Eddies in the River of Time —'

'— *drinking* the River of Time, *reading* the River of Time —'

'— and, in sum, knowing the River of Time as intimately as if she were our Mother — which, in a way, she is, having nourished us all our lives — knowing it rather better, at any rate, than any Insultana of Ott, a place which isn't even *on* the River?'

'Meaning,' concluded the Elephant Drake triumphantly, 'that if we can't tell the real River from these Trillion Fakes, then, my dears, nobody can.'

'There you are, then,' Soraya said to Luka, brazenly taking the credit. 'I told you everything would be taken care of, and taken care of it is going to be.'

Luka decided not to answer her back. It was her flying carpet, after all.

An elephant's trunk is an extraordinary organ. It can smell water from miles away. It can actually smell danger, being able to tell whether approaching strangers are friendly or hostile, and it can smell fear, too. And it can detect very particular scents from long distances: the odours of family members and friends, and of course the sweet smell of home. 'Take us down,' said the Elephant Drake, and the flying carpet, expanded again to a roomier size, flew down towards the labyrinth of waterways. The two Elephant Birds stood at the front with their trunks lifted high in the air, curving downwards at the tips. Luka watched the tips twitch in unison: left, right and left again. It looked like the trunks were dancing with each other, he thought. But could they really smell out the River of Time when they were surrounded by so many other, and no doubt confusing, watery perfumes?

While the Elephant Birds' trunks were dancing, their ears, too, were hard at work, standing rigidly out from their heads and listening for the River's whispers. Water is never silent when it moves. Brooks babble, streams burble, and a larger, slower river has deeper, more complicated things to say. Great rivers speak at low frequencies, too low for human ears to hear, too low even for dogs' ears to pick up their words; and the River of Time told its tales at the lowest frequencies of all, and only elephants' ears could listen to its songs. However, the Elephant Birds' eyes were shut. Elephant eyes are small and dry and don't see very far at all. Eyesight would be of no use in the search for the River of Time.

Time passed. The flying carpet flew across the Trillion and One Forking Paths in long, side-to-side sweeps. The sun sank in the western sky. Everyone felt hungry and thirsty, until Soraya's magic oak chest produced an array of snacks and drinks. 'We're lucky that the Elephant Birds have bird appetites instead of elephant hungers,' Luka thought, 'because elephants eat all the time, and might empty out even that amazing chest.' The shadows of the afternoon lengthened across the landscape. The Elephant Birds said nothing. Luka felt less and less hopeful as the light failed. Maybe this was how the adventure ended, with all his hopes lost in a maze of water. Maybe this – 'That way!' shouted the Elephant Duck, and the Elephant Drake confirmed, 'Definitely, that way, about three miles away.'

Luka ran to stand between them. Their trunks were stretched straight out in front of them now, pointing the way. The carpet came down low over the Forking Paths and accelerated. Trees, shrubs and rivers passed swiftly by beneath them. Then all at once the Elephant Duck called, 'Stop!' and they had arrived.

It was getting dark, and Luka couldn't see what was so different about this particular river, but he hoped with all his might that the Memory Birds were right. 'Down,' said the Elephant Drake. 'We need to touch it, just to be sure.' The carpet flew lower and lower until it was hovering just above the water's surface. The Elephant Duck put the tip of her trunk into the river and then lifted up her head triumphantly. 'Sure!' she shouted, and with cries of happiness both Elephant Birds jumped off the flying carpet into the rediscovered River of Time. 'Home!' they yelled. 'No question! This is the place!' They squirted great jets of River water over each other, and then controlled themselves. The River of Time deserved to be treated with care. It was not a toy. 'Certain,' said the Elephant Drake. 'One hundred per cent.' He gave a little bow. Bear the dog, who prided himself on his own nose, was impressed and, perhaps, a little ashamed that he had not been the one to find the way. Dog the bear was impressed and embarrassed as well, and grumpily neglected to offer the

Memory Birds his congratulations. Nobodaddy seemed lost in thought and didn't say anything, either. 'Thank you, ladies, boys, ordinary-nosed animals, and strange supernatural figures who are, to be honest, a little creepy,' said the Elephant Drake pointedly. 'Thank you all very much. There is no need to applaud.'

Night in the World of Magic can be livelier than the day, depending on your exact location. In Peristan, the Country of Imaginary Beings, the night is when the ogres, the *bhoots*, usually creep about trying to abduct sleeping peris. In the City of Dreams, Khwáb, the night is the time when all its inhabitants' dreams come to life and are acted out in the streets – love affairs, quarrels, monsters, horrors, joys all throng those darkened lanes, and sometimes your dream may, at the night's end, hop into someone else's head, and theirs end up, confusingly, surprisingly, in yours. And in Ott, as Soraya was telling Luka, everyone's behaviour was always naughtiest, wildest and least predictable in the hours between sunset and dawn. Otters ate too much, drank too much, stole their best friends' cars, insulted their grandmothers, and threw rocks at the bronze face of the First King of Ott, her ancestor, whose equestrian statue stood at the palace gate. 'We are a badly behaved people, it's true,' she sighed, 'but we are good at heart.'

In the Trillion and One Forking Paths, however, night was eerily quiet. No bats flew across the face of the moon, no silvery elves glimmered behind bushes, no savage gorgons lurked, waiting to turn the unwary traveller to stone. The silence, the empty hush, was almost frightening. No crickets chirruped, no distant voices called across the water, no nocturnal animals prowled. Soraya, seeing that Luka was a little unnerved by the quiet, tried to inject a note of normalcy into the scene. 'Help me fold this carpet up,' she commanded, adding, in good Otter fashion, 'unless you're too clumsy or ill-mannered, of course.'

They had floated the *Argo* on the River and boarded her. The Memory Birds wouldn't need to pull the vessel – the flying carpet *Resham* could easily do that. But even a magic rug appreciates a few hours' rest, and Soraya on the deck of the *Argo* was putting *Resham* away for the night. Luka took two corners of the soft silken fabric and followed her commands, and saw, to his amazement, that the carpet just went on folding, and folding, and folding as if it were made of folding air. In the end it had folded away into a square no larger or bulkier than a hand-kerchief, and all its enchanted furnishings had vanished with it. 'There,' said Soraya, putting the carpet into a pocket. 'Thank you, Luka.' And then, remembering herself, she added, 'Not that you were really very much use.'

The animals were already asleep. Nobodaddy, who never slept, was behaving as if he was fatigued in a very human sort of way – resting quietly, squatting at the *Argo*'s prow, with his hands wrapped around his legs and his head resting on his knees, still wearing that panama hat. Luka realised that his father must have staged a small recovery, because Nobodaddy was looking slightly more transparent than he had recently. 'Perhaps that's why he's tired,' Luka thought. 'The stronger my father gets, the weaker this Nobodaddy becomes.'

It would be a mistake, Luka knew, to pin too many hopes on this happy reversal. He had heard that ill people sometimes experienced a little misleading 'improvement' before sliding downhill to their . . . to their ends . . . He was feeling very tired himself, but couldn't allow himself to sleep. 'We have to go on,' he said to Soraya. 'Why is everyone behaving as if we have time to spare?'

The stars were out overhead, and they were dancing again, the way they had on the night Rashid fell Asleep, and Luka didn't know if that was a good sign, but he was afraid it might be a bad one. 'Let's go,' he pleaded. But Soraya came towards him and hugged him in a way that wasn't insulting at all, and a moment later he was fast asleep in her arms.

He woke up early, well before dawn, but he wasn't the first to open his eyes. The Memory Birds and animals were still asleep, but Nobodaddy was pacing up and down looking worried (was *that* a good or bad sign? Luka wondered). Soraya was staring towards the far horizon, and if Luka didn't know she was fearless he would have said she was afraid. He went to stand beside her, and to his surprise she took his hand in her own and held it tightly. 'What's the matter?' he asked, and she shook her head violently and did not at first reply. Then in a quiet voice she said, 'I should never have brought you here. This is no place for you.'

Luka answered impatiently, 'It's fine. We're here now. We should get on and find the saving point.'

'And then what?' Soraya asked.

'Then,' Luka stammered, 'then, we'll do whatever comes next.'

'I told you the carpet can't pass through the Great Rings of Fire,' Soraya said. 'But the Heart of Magic, and everything you're looking for, lies beyond them. It's useless. We're lucky to have got this far. I should take you back.'

'About these Rings of Fire –' Luka began.

'Don't ask,' she replied. 'They are immense and impassable, that's all. The Grandmaster makes sure of that.'

'And when you say the Grandmaster –'

'It's just impossible,' she burst out, and there were actual tears in her eyes. 'I'm sorry. It can't be done.'

Nobodaddy had been quiet for a long time, but now he intervened. 'If that is so,' he said, 'the boy probably needs to find it out for himself. And besides, he still has six hundred and fifteen lives to spare, plus one more that he will obviously need to hold on to. And so do his dog and his bear.'

Soraya opened her mouth to argue, but Luka began to bustle about the *Argo*. 'Wake up! Wake up!' he shouted, and the animals grudgingly did as he asked. He turned to Soraya and said firmly, 'To the saving point. Please.'

She nodded her head in surrender. 'Have it your own way,' she said, and took the flying carpet out of her pocket.

There were steel rings at each corner of the carpet, Luka now realised (but had they been there the night before, when *Resham* was being folded up?), and the *Argo* was now attached to these rings by ropes. The Elephant Duck and Elephant Drake took it in turns to sit on the carpet and guide it through the labyrinth of decoy waterways along the true River of Time. And even though the carpet flew swiftly, it was a long journey, and Luka was relieved when he finally saw the golden ball of the saving point up ahead, bobbing up and down like a small buoy. In recognition of the Memory Birds' role as guides, he asked them to punch the ball, and the Elephant Duck jumped into the River and butted the golden orb with her head. The number in the top right-hand corner of Luka's field of vision changed rapidly from 3 to 4, 5 and then 6; but he wasn't paying attention, because the moment the Elephant Duck hit the saving point, the whole world changed, too.

Everything went dark, but night had not fallen. This was some sort of artificial, black, magic darkness, intended to frighten. Then, right in front of them, there arose out of the darkness an immense fireball, billowing up into the sky with a mighty roar, to form a giant flaming wall. 'It goes all the way round the Heart of Magic,' Soraya whispered. 'You're just seeing the front of it from here. That's the first Ring.' Then there was a second and a third roar, each louder than the one before, and two more gigantic rings of flame appeared, the second ring larger than the first and the third larger than the second, so that they could move up and down around the first one, the three forming an impassable triple barrier, like three immense fiery doughnuts in the sky. The colour of the fire, reddish-orange at first, paled quickly until the rings were almost white. 'The hottest fire in existence,' Soraya told Luka. 'White heat. Now do you understand what I've been trying to say?'

Luka understood. If these burning doughnuts encircled the Heart of Magic – the Torrent of Words, the Lake of Wisdom, the Mountain of Knowledge, all of that – then the quest was hopeless. 'This fire,' he said, without much hope, 'the fire the Rings are made of, that isn't the same fire as the Fire of Life – or is it?' Nobodaddy shook his head. 'No,' he said. 'This is the ordinary sort of fire, that turns whatever it touches to ash. The Fire of Life is the only flame that creates – that restores instead of destroying.'

Luka was at a loss for words. He stood on the deck of the *Argo* in the darkness and stared at the sheets of flame. Bear the dog and Dog the bear came to stand in silence on either side of him. And then, without warning, they both began to laugh.

'Ha! Ha! Ha!' barked Bear the dog, and fell down and rolled onto his back and waggled his legs in the air. 'Ha! Ha! Ha! Ha! Ha!' And Dog the bear began to dance a jig on the deck, which made the *Argo* lurch alarmingly from side to side. 'Ho! Ho!' he roared. 'If I hadn't seen it, I wouldn't have believed it. After all that fuss . . . it's just this?'

Soraya was bemused, and even Nobodaddy looked perplexed. 'What on earth are you doing, you foolish beasts?' demanded the Insultana of Ott.

Bear the dog struggled upright, out of breath on account of having laughed so hard. 'But look,' he cried. 'It's Fifi, that's all it is. It's only a great big supersized Fifi, after all this fuss.'

'What are you talking about?' Soraya asked. 'There's no woman out there!'

'Fifi,' giggled Dog the bear. 'The Famous Incredible Fire Illusion of Grandmaster Flame. F-I-F-I, Fifi! That was our name for it in the circus. So Captain Aag is behind all this! We should have known.'

'You know the Grandmaster?' Soraya actually gasped.

'Grandmaster, bah!' answered Bear the dog. 'He was a phoney in the Real World, and he's still a phoney here. These fantastic defences you're so afraid of, they're no defences at all.'

'Fifi is an *illusion*,' explained Dog the bear. 'Smoke and mirrors! She's a magic trick. She isn't really there at all.'

'We'll show you,' said Bear the dog. 'We know how she

works. Put us ashore and we'll put a stop to this silliness once and for all.'

Nobodaddy held up a warning hand. 'Are you sure,' he asked, 'that the Captain Aag of your circus days is the same as the Grandmaster Flame of the Magic World? How can you be certain that these Great Rings of Fire aren't the real thing, even if the circus illusion was a fake?'

'Look up there,' Luka said sharply. 'Where did they appear from?'

Circling in the sky above their heads, horribly illuminated by the giant flames, were seven vultures wearing ruffs around their necks, like European noblemen in old paintings, and also like circus clowns.

That set Bear the dog and Dog the bear off again. 'Ha! Ha!' Dog the bear laughed, jumping off the *Argo* onto the shore. 'Old Aag's beaky buddies just spoiled his trick by flying through it!'

'Ha! Ha!' agreed Bear the dog. 'Watch this, everyone!'

Whereupon they both ran directly at the Great Rings of Fire, and disappeared into the blaze.

Soraya shrieked, and Luka covered his mouth with his hands; and then in a flash the Rings vanished, the light changed, Bear and Dog came running back, the counter in the top right-hand corner of Luka's field of vision *ding*ed up to 7, and the Heart of Magic lay revealed, lit up by the Dawn of Days.

The Heart of Magic – and also Captain Aag, astride a fire-breathing dragon.

6

Into the Heart of Magic

'Is this an illusion, too?' Luka boldly asked Captain Aag. 'Is this another of your pesky magic tricks?' Captain Aag gave what might have been intended as a laugh but came out as a sort of snarl. 'Security,' he said, 'is not an Illusion. Security is the Foundation of any World. Alas! Those of us who labour in the field of Security are often misunderstood, regularly abused, and frequently ignored by those whose safety and values we protect, and yet we struggle on. The Maintenance of Security, young feller-me-lad, is a Thankless Task, I'll have you know; and yet Security must be Maintained. No, Security is not a Deception. It is a Burden, and it has fallen upon me. Fortunately, I do not work alone; and a loyal Fire Bug' – here Luka saw the little telltale flame hovering at Aag's shoulder – 'who makes haste, overcoming all obstacles and distractions, to bring me word that thieves are on their way, a heroic Fire Bug such as we have here, such a Bug is not the creation of flimflam or prestidigitation. Such a Bug is Virtue's Child. Nor is the murderous and terrifying Dragon Nuthog the product of any conjuring trick – as you will soon discover.'

He was a man of hair and anger, this Aag, whose henna-tinted locks stood out from his head like wrathful orange serpents; a man, too, of chin hair, whose russet beard stuck out in all directions like the rays of an ill-tempered sun; a man of eyebrows, quarrelsome scarlet bushes which curled upwards and outwards above a pair of glaring black eyes; and a man also of ear hair, long, stiff, crimson strands of ear hair, that corkscrewed outwards from both those fleshy organs of hearing. Blood-red hair sprouted up from Aag's shirt at the collar and out from his pirate's greatcoat at the cuffs, and Luka imagined the Captain's entire body covered in a luxuriant growth, as if that body were a farm and hair its only crop. Soraya, also a flame-haired person, whispered in Luka's right ear that this Grandmaster's bushy excessivity of hair might give all redheads a bad name.

The hair was Aag's anger made visible. Luka could see that from the way it waved around, shaking itself in his direction as if it were a fist. Why was he so angry? Well, there was the little matter of the destruction of his circus by Luka's curse, that much was obvious; but, in the first place, that circus was now revealed to be a side issue, merely the minor Real World plaything of the Gatekeeper of the Heart of Magic, and, in the second place, that hair had been growing for a long, long time, so Captain Aag had plainly been furious all his life, or, if he was by some chance immortal, then he must have been angry since the beginnings of Time.

'His original name was Menetius,' Nobodaddy whispered into Luka's left ear, 'and he was once the Titan of Rage, until the King of the Gods lost patience with his crosspatchery, killed him with a thunderbolt, and hurled him into the underworld. Eventually he was allowed to return to this lowly job – he's no more than a doorman now – so here he is, in a worse mood than ever, I'm sorry to say.'

The seven vultures had arranged themselves in the air above Aag and the dragon, like guests at a banquet, waiting for a feast. Aag, however, was for a moment in a playful mood. 'In other places, such as the Real World,' he said from the dragon's back, almost as if he were speaking to himself, looking off into the distance and adopting a thoughtful expression, 'such terrible creatures as one might encounter – the Yeti, the Bigfoot, the Unbearably Unpleasant Child – are what I like to call *monsters in space*. There they are, but that's all they are, unchangeable, therefore always the same. Whereas here, where you have no business to be, and where you will very shortly be no more, our monsters can be monsters in time as well; that is to say, they can be one monster after another. Nuthog, here, is actually called *Jaldibadal*, and she's a Magical Chameleon: quite the quick-change artist is old Jaldi when she wants to be, but she's a lazy good-for-nothing creature a lot of the time. Show them, Nuthog, why don't you? There's no real rush to cook them in dragon-fire, after all. The vultures can wait for their lunch.'

Nuthog the dragon – or, more properly, Jaldibadal the Changer – gave what sounded very like a tired, serpentine sigh and then mutated, with what looked very like a monstrous unwilling-ness, into, first, a giant metallic sow, and then, one after the other, a huge, shaggy woman-beast with the tail of a scorpion, a Monstrous Carbuncle (a mirrored creature with a diamond shining out of its head) and an immense mother-tortoise, and finally, with what felt very like a sullen resignation, back into a dragon again. 'Congratulations, Nuthog,' said Captain Aag sarcastically, and his black eyes glittered with anger and his bushy beard flared out around his face like the red flame of an evil match. 'An excellent show. And now, O indolent beast, get on with it and fry these thieves alive before I lose my temper.'

'If my sisters were here beside me, to release me from your spell,' Nuthog spat back, in a voice of considerable sweetness, and in surprising rhyme, 'you wouldn't speak so bravely, and we'd send you back to Hell.'

'Who are her sisters? Where are they?' Luka hissed at Nobodaddy; but then Nuthog blasted the *Argo*, and all the world was flame. 'It's odd, this business of losing a life,' Luka thought. 'You ought to feel something, but you don't.' Then he noticed that the counter in the top left-hand corner of his field of vision had gone down by *fifty lives*. 'I'd better think fast,' he realised, 'or I'll run out of chances right here.' He had re-formed in the same place as before, and so had Bear and Dog. The residents of the World of Magic were unharmed, though Soraya was complaining loudly. 'If I wanted to be sunburned,' she said, 'I would go and sit in the sun. Point that flame-thrower, please, in some other direction.'

Nobodaddy was examining his panama hat, which looked very slightly scorched. 'That's not right,' he grumbled. 'I like this hat.' *BLLLAAARRRTT!* Another blast of dragon-fire, another fifty lives lost. 'Oh, for goodness' sake,' Soraya cried. 'Don't you know that flying carpets are made of delicate stuff?' The Elephant Birds were also extremely upset. 'Memory is a fragile flower,' complained the Elephant Drake. 'It doesn't respond well to heat.'

Things were rapidly arriving at crisis point. 'Nuthog's sisters,' murmured Nobodaddy, 'were imprisoned by the Aalim in blocks of ice, over that way in the Ice Country of Sniffelheim, so that Nuthog would obey Aag's orders.' *BLLLAAARRRTT!* 'That's one hundred and fifty lives gone in no time at all, just four hundred and sixty-five left,' Luka thought as he came back together; and when he looked around him this time, Soraya and the flying carpet had vanished altogether. 'She has abandoned us,' he thought. 'Which means we're done for.'

Just then Dog the bear asked Jaldibadal a question. 'Are you happy?' he demanded, and the monster looked surprised.

'What sort of question is that?' Nuthog asked in return, forgetting to rhyme in her confusion. 'I'm in the process of burning you to death, and this is the thing you want to ask me? What's it to you? Suppose I was happy; would you be happy for me? And if I was not happy, would you sympathise?'

'For example,' persisted Dog the bear, 'are you getting enough to eat? Because I can see your ribs sticking out through your scales.'

'Those aren't my ribs,' answered Nuthog, looking shifty. 'Those are probably the skeletons of the last people I gobbled down.'

'I knew it,' said Dog the bear. 'He's starving you, just as he underfed the animals in the circus. A bony dragon is an even sadder sight than a skinny elephant.'

'Why are you wasting time?' Captain Aag roared from Nuthog's back. 'Get on with it and finish them off.'

'We rebelled against him back in the Real World,' said Bear the dog, 'and he couldn't do a thing about it, and that was the end of him in that place.'

'Cook them!' shouted Captain Aag. 'Grill them, roast them,

123

blast them, toast them! Bear sausages for dinner! Dog chops! Boy cheeks! Cook them and let's eat!'

'It's my sisters,' Nuthog told Bear the dog mournfully. 'As long as they are imprisoned I have no choice but to do as he says.'

'You always have a choice,' said Dog the bear.

'Also,' said a voice from the sky, 'were these perhaps the sisters you were looking for?'

Everyone aboard the *Argo* looked up; and there, high above them, was Queen Soraya of Ott, on King Solomon's magic carpet, *Resham*, which had grown large enough to carry three enormous, shivering monsters, just released from their prison of ice, too cold to fly, too unwell to metamorphose, but alive, and free.

'Bahut-Sara! Badlo-Badlo! Gyara-Jinn!' shouted Nuthog joyfully. The three rescued Changers uttered weak, but happy, moans in reply. Captain Aag had begun to look distinctly panicky on Nuthog's back. 'L-Let's all stay calm now,' he said, stammering a little. 'Let's all remember that I was only following orders, that it was the Aalim, the Guardians of the Fire, who put the three excellent ladies here on ice, and instructed me to work with you, Nuthog, to guard the Gate to the Heart. Let's understand, too, that Security is a hard taskmaster, who requires some tough decisions, and that in consequence it can happen that some innocents suffer for the sake of the greater good. Nuthog, you can understand that, can't you?'

'Only my friends can call me Nuthog,' said Nuthog, and with a smooth little wiggle she flipped Captain Aag off her back. He landed with a bump right under her smoking nose.

'And you're no friend of mine,' Nuthog added, 'so the name is Jaldibadal. And I'm sorry to tell you that, no, I don't understand.'

Captain Aag stood up to face his fate. He looked like a very wretched pirate indeed, all hair and no fire. 'Any last words?' enquired Jaldibadal sweetly. Captain Aag shook his fist at her. 'I'll be back!' he roared.

Jaldibadal shook her scaly head. 'No,' she said, 'I'm afraid you won't.' Then she unleashed an immense flame that wrapped itself around Captain Aag, and when the flame died away there was no more Captain, just a small pile of angry-looking ash.

'Actually, of course,' she added, once Aag had been, so to speak, put out, and his vulture troupe had fled into some distant sky, never to be seen again, 'there are Powers in the Heart that could bring him back to life if they chose. But he doesn't have many friends here, and I think he's probably had his last chance.' She blew hard on the little pile of ash that now lay under her nose, and it was scattered to the four winds. 'Now, young Sir,' she said, looking straight at Luka, 'and, I should say, Sir Dog and Sir Bear, how can I be of assistance?'

Her sisters on the flying carpet flapped their wings experimentally; and found, to their great pleasure, that they could fly again. 'We too will help you,' said Badlo-Badlo the Changer, and Bahut-Sara and Gyara-Jinn nodded their assent. The Insultana Soraya clapped her hands in delight. 'That's more like it,' she rejoiced. 'We've got an army now.'

In all the excitement nobody noticed a small fiery Bug rushing away from them as quickly as it could fly, making its way deep into the Heart of Magic, whooshing along as quickly as a wildfire running before a helpful wind.

Nobodaddy was acting strangely, Luka thought. He was fidgety, scratching constantly at his panama hat's scorched brim. He seemed irritable, pacing up and down and rubbing his hands together and speaking in monosyllables, when he spoke at all. Sometimes he seemed almost transparent and at other times almost solid, so plainly Rashid Khalifa at home in Kahani was struggling for life and health, and maybe that struggle was having a bad effect on Nobodaddy's mood. But Luka began to have other suspicions. Maybe Nobodaddy had just been humouring him, toying with him for his own warped amusement. Who knew what sort of twisted sense of humour such a creature might have? Maybe he had never expected Luka to get this far, and in fact didn't like the idea that they were now flying towards the Fire of Life itself. Maybe he hadn't been honest, and didn't want the quest to succeed. He'd need watching carefully, Luka decided, in case he tried to sabotage everything at the last moment. He looked, walked and talked like the Shah of Blah, but that didn't make him Luka's father. Maybe Bear and Dog had been right: Nobodaddy was not to be trusted an inch. Or maybe there was an argument raging inside him, maybe the Rashid-ness he had absorbed was at war with the death-creature that did the absorbing. Maybe dying was always like this: an argument between death and life.

'Who wins that argument is a matter for another day,' Luka thought. 'Right now, I've got to stop thinking of him as my dad.'

Soraya's flying carpet was aloft again, after briefly landing to allow all the travellers, and the *Argo* of course, to come aboard. Jaldi, Sara, Badlo and Jinn, the four Changers, in their dragon shapes, flew in strict formation around the *Resham*, one on each of the carpet's four sides, protecting it against any possible attack. Luka looked down and saw below him the River of Time flowing from the distant, and invisible, Lake of Wisdom at the Heart of the Heart (which was still too far away to be seen) – the River flowing into, and then out of, the immense Circle of the Circular Sea, at the bottom of which, he knew, slept the giant Worm Bottomfeeder, who coiled his body all the way around the Circle just so that his head could nibble at his tail. Outside the Circle, directly beneath the flying carpet at that moment, were the vast territories of the Badly Behaved Gods – the gods in whom nobody believed any longer, except as stories that people once liked to tell.

'They don't have any power in the Real World any more,' Rashid Khalifa used to say, sitting in his favourite squashy armchair, with Luka curled up on his lap, 'so there they all are in the World of Magic, the ancient gods of the North, the gods of Greece and Rome, the South American gods, and the gods of Sumeria and Egypt long ago. They spend their time, their infinite, timeless time, pretending they are still divine, playing all their old games, fighting their ancient wars over and over again, and trying to forget that nobody really cares about them these days, or even remembers their names.'

'That's pretty sad,' Luka said to his father. 'To be honest with you, the Heart of Magic sounds a lot like an old folks' home for washed-up superheroes.'

'Don't let them hear you say that,' Rashid Khalifa replied, 'because they all look gorgeous and youthful and luminous and, well, perfect. Being divine, or even ex-divine, has its perks. And inside the Magic World they still have the use of their superpowers. It's in the Real World that their thunderbolts and enchantments no longer have any effect.'

'It must be awful for them,' Luka said, 'to have been worshipped and adored for so long, and then just discarded, like last year's unfashionable clothes.'

'Particularly for the Aztec deities from Mexico,' Rashid said, putting on his scary voice. 'Because they were used to receiving human sacrifices; the throats of living people were cut and their lifeblood flowed into the gods' stone goblets. Now there's no blood for those disused gods to drink. You've heard of vampires? Most of them are blood-thirsty, long-in-the-tooth, undead Aztec gods. Huitzilopochtli! Tezcatlipoca! Tlahuizcalpantecuhtli! Macuilcoz-cacuauhtli! Itztlacoliuhqui-Ixquimilli —'

'Stop, stop,' Luka begged. 'No wonder people stopped worshipping them. Nobody could pronounce their names.'

'Or it may be because they all behaved so badly,' Rashid said.

This got Luka's attention. The notion of gods behaving badly was an odd one. Weren't gods supposed to set an example to the people whose gods they were? 'Not in the Olden Days,' Rashid said. 'These Olden, and now Jobless, gods usually behaved as badly as people, or actually much worse, because, being gods, they could behave badly on a bigger scale. They were selfish, rude, meddlesome, vain, bitchy, violent, spiteful, lustful, gluttonous, greedy, lazy, dishonest, tricky and stupid, and all of it exaggerated to the maximum, because they had those

128

superpowers. When they were greedy they could swallow a city, and when they were angry they could drown the world. When they meddled in human lives they broke hearts, stole women and started wars. When they were lazy they slept for a thousand years, and when they played their little tricks other people suffered and died. Sometimes a god would even kill another god by knowing his weak spot and going for it, the way a wolf goes for the throat of its prey.'

'Maybe it's a good thing they faded away,' Luka said, 'but it must make the Heart of Magic a peculiar sort of place.'

'Nowhere more peculiar in the universe,' Rashid replied.

'And what about the gods people still believe in?' Luka asked. 'Are they in the Heart of Magic as well?'

'Oh, dear me, no,' said Rashid Khalifa. 'They're all still right here with us.'

The memory of Rashid faded away, and Luka found himself flying over a phantasmagoric landscape dotted with broken columns and statuary, with creatures out of fable and legend walking, running and flying among them. There – over there! – were two vast and trunkless legs of stone, the last remaining echoes of Ozymandias, King of Kings. Here, slouching towards them, was an immense rough beast, Sphinx-like, only male, and spotted, a man with a hyena's body and its hideous laugh as well, destroying whatever house or temple, hill or tree it passed, by the sheer force of its ecstatic, ruinous laughter. And there! – yes, right there! – was the Sphinx herself! Yes, surely that was she! The Lion with the Woman's Head! See how she stopped strangers and insisted on talking to them . . . 'It's too bad,' said Soraya. 'She keeps asking everyone the same old riddle, and nobody can be bothered to answer, because everybody has known it for ever. She really needs to get a new act.'

A gigantic egg walked by below them on long, yolk-coloured legs. A winged unicorn flew past. A curious three-part creature – a crocodile, lion and hippopotamus combined – shuffled its way towards the Circular Sea. The sight of a small god in the shape of a dog excited Bear. 'That is Xolotl,' warned Soraya. 'Stay away from him. He's the god of bad luck.' That disappointed Bear the dog a good deal. 'Why does Bad Luck turn out to be a dog?' he complained. 'In the Real World, a faithful dog is very good luck for its owner. No wonder these bad-luck gods are done for.'

Luka couldn't help noticing that the Heart of Magic was in some disrepair. The Egyptians' pyramids were crumbling, and in the Nordic quarter a gigantic ash tree lay on its side, its three huge roots clutching at the sky. And if those meadows over in that direction were really the Elysian Fields, where the souls of great heroes lived on for ever, why was the grass so brown? 'These places are in really bad shape,' Luka said, and Soraya nodded sadly. 'Magic is fading from the universe,' she said. 'We aren't needed any more, or that's what you all think, with your High Definitions and low expectations. One of these days you'll wake up and we'll be gone, and then you'll find out what it's like to live without even the idea of Magic. But Time moves on, and there isn't a thing we can do about it. Would you like,' she said, brightening, 'to see the Battle of the Beauties? I believe this is the right time of day.'

The carpet began to fly down towards a great pavilion topped by seven golden, onion-shaped domes, all shining in the morning sun. 'Shouldn't we stay out of these gods' and goddesses' way, though?' Luka objected. 'Surely we don't want them to see us, to know we're here? We are thieves, after all.'

'They can't see you,' Soraya answered. 'If you're from the Real World, they are blind to your existence. You don't exist for them, just as they no longer exist for you. You can walk right up to any number of gods or goddesses, say "boo" and pinch their noses, and they'll act as if nothing happened, or as if they're being bothered by a fly. As for persons from the general neighbourhood, like myself, they don't care about us. We aren't part of their stories, so they think we don't count. Stupid of them, but that's the way they are.'

'Then it's a sort of ghost town,' Luka thought, 'and these supposed almighties are sort of sleepwalkers, or echoes of themselves. It's like a mythological theme park here – you could call it Godland – only there are no visitors, except for us, and we've come to pilfer a piece of their most precious possession.' To Soraya he said, 'But if they can't see us, won't it be easy to steal the Fire of Life? In which case, shouldn't we just hurry up and do it?'

'In the Heart of the Heart, which is to say inside the Circular Sea, where the Lake of Wisdom is bathed in the Eternal Dawn,' said Soraya, 'things are very different. There are none of these moronic sleepwalking sacked gods in there. That is the Country of the Aalim – the Three Jos – who watch over the whole of Time. They are the Ultimate Guardians of the Fire, and they don't miss a thing.'

'The Three Jos?' asked Luka.

'Jo-Hua, Jo-Hai and Jo-Aiga,' Soraya answered, and she was

whispering now. 'What Was, What Is and What Will Come. The Past, the Present and the Future. The Possessors of All Knowledge. The Aalim: the Trinity of Time.'

The golden onion domes were right below them now, but Luka was thinking only of the Fire of Life. 'So how do we get past the Jos, then?' he whispered back to Soraya, and she spread her arms with a shrug and a rueful smile. 'You knew from the start,' she said, 'that no one has ever done it. But there's somebody who usually skulks around here, who may be able to help us. He usually lies pretty low, but this is the best place to find him. When the Beauties battle, he likes to watch.'

She landed the flying carpet behind a spreading thicket of rhododendrons, large enough to conceal the *Argo*. 'Few magical creatures ever approach a rhododendron,' she told Luka, 'because they believe them to be poisonous. If there were any Yetis in the neighbourhood they would devour them, of course, but this is not Abominable Snowman country, and so the *Argo* will be safe enough here for a while.' Then she folded up the carpet, put it in her pocket, and marched towards the onion-domed building. The four Changers shape-shifted into metal sows, and, clanking a good deal, trotted along beside Soraya, Nobodaddy, Luka, the Memory Birds, Bear the dog and Dog the bear towards the Battle Pavilion, from which loud, angry noises could be heard: the sounds of goddesses at war.

'It's so idiotic,' Soraya said. 'They fight over which of them is the loveliest, as if it mattered. Beauty goddesses are the worst. They have been flattered and spoiled for thousands of years, mortals and immortals have sacrificed their lives for them, and as a result you wouldn't believe the things they believe they are entitled to. Nothing but the best will do for them, and if it belongs to someone else, so what? They are sure they deserve it more than its owner, whether it's a jewel or a palace or a man. But now here they are in the junkyard of their power, and their beauty no longer launches warships or makes men die for love, so there's nothing left to do but fight each other over a hollow crown, a title that means nothing: *the loveliest of them all*.'

'But that's you – you are the loveliest of them all,' Luka wanted to tell her. 'See how your red hair flies in the wind, and then there's the perfection of your eyes, your face, and I even enjoy it when you're insulting people, and I don't like it when you sound sad.' Unfortunately he was too shy to say such embarrassing words out loud, and then a great burst of cheering began, and grew louder and louder, so she wouldn't have been able to hear anything anyway.

The crowd in the pavilion was the sort of gathering of fantastic creatures out of fables and legends which would have utterly astounded Luka just a few days ago, but which he had, by now, almost begun to expect. 'Oh, look, there are fauns here – horned, goat-eared and goat-hoofed – and proud centaurs stamping their feet,' he thought, and was surprised by how unsurprising the World of Magic was starting to feel. 'And winged men – would those be *angels*? – angels watching women fight? – that doesn't sound right. And presumably all these other battle fans are the lower orders of the various god gangs, the gods' servants and children and pets, out for a morning's fun.'

Just then, the first goddess was ejected from the fray. She came tumbling head over heels through the air, right over Luka's head, screaming her rage as she went by, and turning from a palely powdered, geisha-like beauty into a hideous long-toothed harridan and then back into the geisha again. She crashed through the swing doors of the fight hall and was gone. 'I believe that was the Japanese *rasetsu*, Kishimojin,' said Nobodaddy, with the air of a goddess-fight connoisseur. (Being at the battle had clearly improved his mood.) 'A *rasetsu* is more demon than goddess, really, as you saw from her transformations just then. Out of her class in this company, one feels; you'd expect her to be the first one to be knocked out.'

As Kishimojin retreated from the pavilion, Luka could still hear her high-pitched cursing. '*May your heads split into seven pieces like the flower of the basil shrub.*' 'The so-called Arjaka curse,' Nobodaddy explained to Luka. 'Terrifying in the Real World, but pathetically ineffective against these formidable females.'

Luka couldn't see much of the fight, but didn't like to ask any of his companions to lift him up. Over the heads of the crowd he saw thunderbolts being hurled and loud explosions lighting up the fighting area. He saw huge clouds of butterflies and flocks of birds, apparently also at war with one another. 'There's a little side battle going on between Mylitta, the moon goddess of ancient Sumer, and the Aztec vampire queen Xochiquetzal,' Nobodaddy reported. 'They don't like it that they both have bird and butterfly entourages – beauty goddesses always want to be unique! – so they usually go at each other right away, and so do their flapping friends. Usually the two ladies knock each other out and leave the field clear for the top girls.'

The Roman love goddess, Venus, was eliminated early, staggering from the hall, reattaching her severed arms as she went.

'The Romans are low down in the rankings here in the Heart of Magic,' Nobodaddy shouted over the din. 'For a start, they are homeless. Their followers never came up with an Olympus or Valhalla for them, so they wander around the place looking, to be frank, like vagrants. Also, everybody knows they are just imitations of the Greeks, and who wants to watch second-rate remakes when you can see the original movies for free?'

Luka shouted back that he didn't know there was a divine pecking order. 'Who's at the top of it, then?' he yelled. 'Which bunch of ex-gods are the Top Gods?' 'I'll tell you which ones are the snootiest,' Nobodaddy shouted. 'The Egyptians, for sure. And in these battles their girl Hathor often comes out on top.'

On this occasion, however, it was the Greek Cypriot, Aphrodite, who was the last goddess standing. After Ishtar of Babylon and Freya, Queen of the Valkyries, had beaten each other unconscious in the mud-wrestling ring, the betting favourite, cow-eared Hathor – a shape-shifter like Jaldi and her sisters, only far more powerful, capable of turning herself into clouds and stones – had made the mistake of turning briefly into a fig tree, which had allowed Aphrodite to chop her down. So at the end of the battle it was Aphrodite who approached the great Mirror that was the Ultimate Arbiter of Beauty, and asked the famous question, *Mirror, Mirror on the Wall*, and so on; Aphrodite it was who received the Mirror's accolade, *You are the loveliest*, as was traditional. 'Oh well,' said Nobodaddy, 'it's good exercise, and they'll all be back at it tomorrow. There's not that much for them to do around here. It's not as if they can stay home and watch TV, or go out to the gym.'

The victor, Aphrodite, passed through the crowd, waving

graciously, but a little robotically. She was within a few feet of Luka at one point, and he saw that her eyes were oddly glazed, and focused on infinity. 'No wonder she can't see anyone Real,' he thought. 'She has eyes only for herself.'

He looked around for Soraya, but she had disappeared. 'She probably got bored,' said Nobodaddy. 'We'll find her outside.' As they left the Battle Hall, he pointed out some of the more remarkable audience members to Luka. The Humbaba of Assyria was a naked, scaly giant with a horned head and lion's paws. His tail was a living snake with a little, flicking forked tongue. 'And so is his willy,' Luka noted with delight. 'That's quite something, a willy-snake, that's a thing I've never seen before.' And close behind this brand-new sight was a group of Central Asian Boramez, who looked like baby lambs, except that their legs were made of two different varieties of long. fleshy roots, like sweet potatoes and parsnips. 'Lamb chops and two veg,' Luka thought. 'Yum! These creatures would make a complete, nourishing meal.' There were several three-headed trolls in the crowd, and many disappointed Valkyries, who had been hoping for their girl Freya to come out on top. '*Nev*-er *mind*,' they told one another in their sing-song, phlegmatic, good-natured Nordic way, 'to-*morr*-ow *is* an-*oth*-er *day*.'

Soraya was waiting in front of the rhododendron bushes, looking innocent, which was such an unusual look for her that Luka immediately suspected she was up to something. 'What's going on?' he began, then changed tack. 'Never mind,' he continued. 'We're wasting time. Let's get going, okay?'

'Once upon a time,' said Soraya dreamily, 'there was an Indian tribe called the Karaoke. They didn't have Fire, so they were sad and cold and never sang a note.'

'This is no time for fairy tales,' said Luka, but Soraya ignored him and continued. 'Fire had been created by a god-type creature named Ekoarak,' she said in the same dreamy, musical voice, which Luka had to admit was a beautiful voice, a voice exactly like his mother's voice, which made it comforting to listen to, 'but he had hidden it in a music box and given it, for safe keeping, to two old witches, with instructions that on no account were they to give it to the Karaoke –'

'There's a point in here somewhere, I hope,' Luka interrupted, a little rudely, but that only made the Insultana smile, for, after all, it was the Otter way.

'Coyote was the one who decided he would steal the Fire,' she said. Bear the dog perked up. 'This is a story about a heroic prairie dog?' he said hopefully. Soraya ignored him. 'He got the Lion, the Big Bear, the Little Bear, the Wolf, the Squirrel and the Frog to help him. They spaced themselves out between the witches' tent and the Karaoke village and waited. Coyote told one Karaoke Indian to visit the witches and attack their tent. When he did so they came out with their broomsticks and ran after him to chase him away. Coyote ran inside, opened the box with his nose, stole the burning firebrand, and ran. When the witches saw him running with the Fire they forgot about the Indian and chased Coyote instead. Coyote ran like the wind, and when he was tired he passed the burning wood to the Lion, who ran as far as the Big Bear, who ran on to the Little Bear, and so on. Finally the Frog swallowed the Fire and dived under the river where the witches couldn't follow him, and then he jumped out on the far bank of the river and spat the Fire out onto dry wood in the Karaoke village, and the Fire crackled and burned and the flames rose high into the sky, and everybody cheered. Soon afterwards the Indian returned, having gone into the witches' tent (while they were chasing Coyote) and stolen the whole music box, and after that the Karaoke village was warm, and everyone sang all the time, because the magical music box never stopped playing its selection of popular songs.'

'Okay . . . y . . . y,' said Luka doubtfully. 'It's a nice enough story, but . . .'

Coyote strolled out from behind the rhododendron bushes, looking Wild and Western and ready for trouble. *Buenas dias, kid*, he said, in a cool, slanting sort of way. *My friend here, that's the Insultana, indicated you could probly use some help. You ask me, I reckon you need all the help you can git.* He gave a confident, wolfish laugh. *Hear this, Fire Thief. Aint nobody got more sperience than me in the fire-stealin line, xceptin maybe one individual – big individual he was, too – but after what happen to him last time aroun, he aint available. Caint be helped. Reckon he lost his nerve.*

'What happened?' Luka asked, not really wanting to know.

Taken, said Coyote, bluntly. *Got his big self tied down on a rock. Si, señor. Spreadeagled on there at the mercy of the merciless. Eagle got to chewin on his liver all day, which liver then done fix itself up an grow back ever' night on account of 3-J magic, so that Eagle he could jus go on munchin till the end of time. You want more?*

'No, thank you,' Luka said, thinking, not for the first time, that he was a long, long way out of his depth. But he made his voice sound a lot braver than he felt and went on. 'Also,' he said, 'I'm smelling a rat, to be honest with you. Everybody has been telling me all along that the Fire has never been stolen in the whole history of the World of Magic. Now you tell me that you stole it, Coyote, and apparently this old-timer you're talking about stole it, too? So what's the truth? Has everyone been lying to me this whole time, and it's actually easier to steal the Fire than anyone has admitted?'

Soraya replied, 'We should have explained things better to you. Nobodaddy should have done it right at the outset, and so should I. You're right to feel aggrieved. So this is the truth of it. The World of Magic has taken many forms in different times and places, and it has had many different names. It has changed its location, its geography and its laws, as the history of the Real World has moved from age to age. In several of those times and places, it's true, Fire Thieves did make successful runs at the Fire of the Gods. But nobody has succeeded since the Heart of Magic assumed its current shape and form, in this place, in this time, here and now. That's the truth. The Aalim have always been around – after all, there's no escape from the Past, the Present and the Future, is there? – but for a long time they left the management of things to the gods of the period, the same ex-gods you see here, inefficient deities who didn't always do such a good job. Now the Aalim have taken control of matters themselves. Everything has been reordered. The Fire of Life is impregnably defended. The Three Jos know everything. Jo-Hua knows even the smallest details of the Past, Jo-Hai can see even the smallest incident in the Present, and Jo-Aiga can foretell the Future. Nobody has managed to steal the Fire since they took charge.'

'Oh,' said Luka, feeling horribly deflated, because the notion that Nobodaddy and Soraya and everyone else had hidden from him the successful Thefts of Fire had briefly given him hope. If Coyote could do it, he had thought, then he could do it, too. But that short-lived burst of optimism fizzled out and died like a well-doused fire as Soraya explained the truth. He turned back towards Coyote, humbly. 'What sort of help did you have in mind?' he asked.

This beautiful lady here she's kindly disposed to you and I'm indebted to her for old kindnesses, said Coyote, chewing something at the side of his mouth. *She says maybe I could guide you through the inner country, which maybe I could at that. Says maybe you'll need somebody to make a* carrera de distracción. *That's a decoy run. Says I should see if I can get the old gang together and run that diversion for you while you make your crazy bid. Wants me to draw the 3–J attention way from you while you run for glory.*

Then Soraya said something that drained all the hope out of Luka's body. 'I can't take you in there,' she said. 'Into Aalim country If they see the Flying Carpet of King Solomon the Wise entering their space, and if they become aware of *him –*' here she nodded her head at Nobodaddy with a distasteful expression on her face – 'and, believe me, they will become aware, then the game will be up right away; they'll smell trouble and come down on us with all the power they have, and I'm not strong enough to fight them off for very long. That's why I wanted to find Coyote. I want you to have a plan.'

'I'm going with you,' said Bear the dog, loyally.

'I'm going too,' said Dog the bear in a gruff, big-brotherish voice. 'Somebody has to look after you.'

The Memory Birds shuffled their webbed feet awkwardly.

'It's not really our thing, fire-stealing,' said the Elephant Duck. 'We just remember stuff, that's all. We're just rememberers.' And the Elephant Drake added clumsily, 'We'll always remember you.'

The Elephant Duck gave him a furious look. 'What he means,' she said, nudging her partner roughly, 'is that we'll wait with Queen Soraya for your return.'

The Elephant Drake harrumphed. 'Obviously,' he said. 'I misspoke, obviously. We'll obviously be waiting. Obviously, that is what I meant to say.'

Nobodaddy squatted down so that he could look Luka in the eye. 'She's right,' he said, annoying Luka intensely by using Rashid Khalifa's most serious and loving voice. 'I can't go with you. Not in there.'

'Here's something else you should have told me before now,' Luka said angrily. 'Both of you. How am I supposed to do this without you?'

Jaldibadal the Changer said firmly, 'You still have us.'

Nuthog's sisters had fully recovered from their icy ordeal by now, and nodded enthusiastically, which made their metal pig ears clank against the sides of their heads. 'We are creatures of the Heart,' said Badlo-Badlo – at least Luka thought it was Badlo, but with all their Changing it was hard to remember which of the four sisters was which. 'That's right,' said – maybe – Bahut-Sara. 'The Three Jos will not suspect us.'

'Thank you,' said Luka gratefully, 'but maybe you could change back into dragons? Dragons might be more useful than metal pigs if we come under attack.' The quadruple transformation was quickly completed, and Luka was pleased to see that there were differences in their colouring which made it easier to tell the Changers apart: Nuthog (Jaldi) was the red dragon, Badlo the green one, Sara the blue one, and Gyara-Jinn, the Changer with eleven possible transformations, the largest of the four, was golden.

'Then it's settled,' Luka said. 'Bear, Dog, Jaldi, Sara, Badlo, Jinn and me. Seven of us, into the Heart of the Heart.'

'Call me Nuthog,' said Nuthog. 'We're friends now. And I never liked my real name much anyhow.'

Coyote spat out the remnant of his dinner and cleared his throat. *Aint you forgettin somethin here, chico? Or is it your intent to insult me by declinin my offer in public an in spite of it being both generous an bona fide? An in spite of your ignorance and my particular expertise?*

Luka was genuinely unsure how to reply. This Coyote was a friend of Soraya's, so that made him trustworthy, Luka supposed, but was he really necessary? Maybe the best way was just to creep in without doing anything to draw the Aalim's attention in any direction at all, even the wrong one?

'Just tell me one thing,' he said, rounding on Nobodaddy, who he was beginning to dislike more and more, 'how many levels do I still have to get through? I've got this single-digit counter up here on the right, saying Seven —'

'Seven is excellent,' said Nobodaddy. 'Seven is actually impressive. But you won't complete Level Eight unless you do succeed in stealing the Fire of Life —'

'Which, let's be clear, has never been done — at least, not in the current format of the Magical World,' interjected Luka crossly. 'Not under the Rules of the Game that are presently in effect.'

'And Level Nine is the longest and hardest of all,' Nobo-daddy added. 'That's the one in which you have to get all the way back to the Start and jump back into the Real World without being caught. Oh, and you will have the entire World of Magic up in arms and chasing after you, by the way. That's Level Nine.'

'Wonderful. Thanks a lot,' said Luka.

'You're welcome,' said Nobodaddy in a cold, hard voice. 'I seem to recall that this was your idea. I distinctly recall your saying, "Let's go." Was I perhaps mistaken?' That wasn't Luka's father talking at all. That was a creature who was trying to suck his father's life away. Luka suspected even more strongly than before that this whole adventure had just been Nobodaddy's way of passing the time until his real work was done. It has just been *something to do*.

'No,' said Luka. 'No, there was no mistake.'

Just then he heard a loud noise.

A loud, *loud*, LOUD noise.

In fact, to call this noise 'loud' was like saying that a tsunami was just a big wave. To describe how loud this loudness was, Luka thought, he would have to say, for example, that if the Himalayas were made of sound instead of stone and ice then this noise would have been Mount Everest; or maybe not Everest, but definitely one of the Eight Thousand Metre Peaks. Luka had learned from Rashid Khalifa, the least mountaineering of men, but a man who liked a good list, that there were four-teen Eight Thousand Metre Peaks on Earth: in descending order, Everest, K2, Kanchenjunga, Lhotse, Makalu, Cho Oyu, Dhaulagiri, Manaslu, Nanga Parbat, Annapurna, Gasherbrum I,

Broad Peak, Gasherbrum II and the beautiful Xixabangma Feng. It wasn't so easy to list his Fourteen Loudest Sounds, Luka thought, but he was quite sure this one was in the top three. So it was at the Kanchenjunga level, at the very least.

The sound went on, and on, and on, and Luka covered his ears. All around them pandemonium had broken out in the Heart of Magic. Crowds were running in all directions, flying creatures were taking to the air, swimming things to the water, riders to their horses. It was a general mobilisation, Luka thought, and then in a flash he understood what the sound was. It was a call to arms.

The game just changed, muchacho, Coyote trotted over to shout in Luka's ear. *You need help now, big time. Aint nobody heard that noise round here in hunnerds of years. That's the Big Noise. That's the Fire Alarm.*

'It must have been that Fire Bug who raised the Alarm,' Luka realised at once, disgusted with himself for having forgotten about that little tale-telling flame, the World of Magic's tiniest Security operative, but, it seemed, one of the most dangerous. 'It was hovering by Captain Aag's shoulder and then it disappeared. We didn't pay attention to it, and now we're paying the price for our carelessness.'

At long last the siren of the Fire Alarm died down, but the hysterical activity all around them became, if anything, even more frenzied. Soraya dragged Luka behind the rhododendron bushes. 'When the Fire Alarm sounds it means two things,' she said. 'It means that the Aalim know that someone is trying to steal the Fire of Life. And it means that all the residents of the Heart of Magic are rendered capable of seeing intruders until the All-Clear, which doesn't sound until the thief is caught.'

'You mean everyone can see me now?' Luka said in horror. 'And Bear and Dog as well?' When they heard that, the dog and the bear ran and hid behind the rhododendrons as well. Soraya nodded. 'Yes,' she said. 'There's only one course of action. You must abandon your plan, and climb aboard *Resham*, and I will fly as high as I can rise and as fast as I can ride and I will try to get you back to the Starting Point before they find you, because if they catch you they may Perminate all three of you on the spot, without asking for an explanation of your presence or giving a reason for their drastic measures. Or else they'll put you on trial and Perminate you after that. The adventure is over, Luka Khalifa. It's time to go home.'

Luka was silent for a long moment. Then he said simply, 'No.'

Soraya smacked her forehead with the palm of her hand. 'Backchat he's giving me now. "No," he says. Tell me your grand plan, hero boy. No, no! Let me guess! You're going to take on all the gods and monsters of the Heart of Magic, with a dog, a bear and four dragons as the sum total of your attack force; and you're going to steal what has never been stolen, what nobody has tried to steal for hundreds of years, and then you're going to get home? How? I'm supposed to wait around and give you a ride, is that it? Well, by all means. Go right ahead. That masterly scheme sounds like it will definitely work.'

'You're almost right,' Luka said. 'But you forgot I'll have Coyote's decoy run helping me as well.'

Hold it, chico, said Coyote, looking alarmed. *Hold it there one minute. Didn I say the game jus changed? That offer aint no longer on the table.*

'Listen,' said Luka. 'What do thieves do when the Fire Alarm sounds?'

They run for their life. Aint nobody done it for hunnerds of years but that's what they done then. Warnt no use. Even the old Titan back in the day, he got taken an tied to a rock and an old vulture started chewin –

'Eagle,' said Luka. 'You said it was an eagle.'

'Pinions differ as to the species of bird. Aint no doubt about the chewin.

'So,' said Luka determinedly, 'running isn't any use, unless you run in an unexpected direction. And, now that the Fire Alarm has sounded, which is the one direction in which nobody will expect us to flee?'

Nobodaddy was the one who answered Luka's question. 'Towards the Fire of Life,' he said. 'Into the Heart of the Heart. Towards the danger. You're right.'

'Then,' said Luka, 'that's the way we're going.'

146

7

The Fire of Life

The whole World of Magic was on Red Alert. Jackal-headed Egyptian deities, fierce scorpion- and jaguar-men, giant one-eyed, man-eating Cyclopes, flute-playing centaurs, whose pipes could entice strangers into cracks in rocks where they would be imprisoned for all time, Assyrian treasure-nymphs made of gold and jewels, whose precious bodies could tempt thieves into their poisoned whipcord nets, flying griffins with lethal claws, flightless basilisks glaring in all directions with their deadly eyes, Valkyries on cloud-horses in the sky, bull-headed minotaurs, slithering snake-women; and huge rocs – larger than the one that bore Sinbad the Sailor to its nest – charged wildly across the land and through the air, answering the Fire Alarm, hunting, hunting. In the Circular Sea, after the Alarm sounded, mermaids rose from the waters singing siren songs to lure the foul intruders to their doom. Enormous island-sized creatures – krakens, zaratans and monstrous rays – hung motionless on the Sea's surface; if an intruder were to pause on the back of one of the beasts for a rest, it would dive and drown him, or flip over to reveal its giant mouth and its sharp triangular teeth, and swallow the trespasser down in bite-sized chunks. And most terrible of all was the gigantic Worm Bottomfeeder, who rose blind and roaring from the Sea's usually silent depths, in a rage to consume the scoundrels who had triggered the Fire Alarm and disturbed its two-thousand-year sleep.

Amid the chaos of that World the Fire Gods rose in all their majesty to defend Vibgyor, the One Bridge to the Heart of the Heart, the rainbow arch that crossed the sundering Sea and enabled the favoured few to enter the Aalim's lands. Amaterasu, the Japanese sun goddess, emerged from the cave where she had sulked for two millennia after quarrelling with her brother, the storm god, with the magic sword Kusanagi in her hand, and rays of sunlight flying outwards from her head like spears. Beside her was the flaming child Kagutsuchi, whose burning birth had killed his mother, Izanami the Divine. And Surtr with his fiery sword and at his elbow his female companion, Sinmara, also bearing a lethal sword of fire. And Irish Bel. And Polynesian Mahuika with her fingernails of flame. And lame Hephaestus, the smith of Olympus, with his pale Roman echo Vulcan at his side. And Inti of the Incas, the Sun with the Human Face, and the Aztec Tonatiuh, thirsty for blood, Tonatiuh the former Lord of the Fifth World, to please whom twenty thousand people used to be sacrificed each year. And towering above them all like a giant pillar in the sky was falcon-headed Ra of Egypt, his piercingly sharp bird-eyes searching for the would-be thieves, with the Bennu bird sitting on his shoulder, the grey heron that was the Egyptian phoenix, and his mighty weapons, the wadjets, the disks of the sun, held urgently in his hands. These great colossi guarded the Bridge and waited with clouds at their foreheads and murder in their eyes.

Inhabitants of the Heart of Magic rushed freely across the Bridge in both directions, hunting, hunting; but for the hunted intruders, Luka thought, there appeared to be no way past the falcon eyes of Ra. Luka, hiding with his companions behind the rhododendron bushes, had the feeling that the thicket was shrinking, dwindling away and becoming a less and less adequate shelter. His heart was beating too rapidly. Things were definitely getting scary.

'The good thing about all these ex-gods,' said Soraya comfortingly, 'is that they're all stuck in their old stories. I'm sure the Fire Bug will have reported accurately to the Aalim – *a boy, a dog, a bear*, he will have said – but when the Fire Alarm goes off, everyone here inevitably starts hunting for the Usual Suspects.'

'Who are the Usual Suspects?' Luka wanted to know. He realised he was whispering, and that he wished Soraya would lower her voice as well.

'Oh, the ones who were Fire Thieves in the times and places in which these gods were the gods,' Soraya said, waving an arm airily. '*You* know. Or,' she added, reverting to her old Insultana habits, 'maybe you're too ignorant. Maybe your father didn't teach you as much as he should have. Maybe he didn't know himself.' Then, seeing the expression on Luka's face, she softened her voice and relented. 'The Algonquin Indians got Rabbit to steal Fire for them,' she said, 'and you know about Coyote already. Beaver and Nanabozho the Shape-Shifter did the same for other tribes. Possum tried and failed, but then Grandmother Spider stole Fire for the Cherokee in a clay urn, which reminds me' – Soraya paused for a moment – 'that you will need this.'

She was holding a little clay pot in her hands. Luka looked inside it. A small group of what looked like half a dozen black potatoes nestled on a bed of twigs. 'This,' said Soraya, 'is one of the famous Ott Pots, and there inside it are a few of the famous Ott Potatoes. Once the Fire of Life touches them, they'll burn brightly, and they won't easily be put out.' She hung the pot around his neck by its leather strap. 'Where was I?' She thought for a minute, then resumed. 'Oh yes. Maui – that's Maui-tikitiki-a-Taranga to you – stole Fire from the fingernails of the fire goddess Mahuika and gave it to the Polynesians. *She'll* definitely be on the lookout for *him*. And so on.'

You neglected to include the First Thief, Coyote said. *Oldest and greatest. King of the Hill. Inspiration to us all. Stole it for all mankind.*

'The Titan Prometheus,' Soraya said, 'was the brother, oddly enough, of your friend, the late, unlamented Captain Aag. Not that they ever got on. Couldn't stand each other, in fact. Anyhow: three million four hundred thousand years ago the Old Boy was indeed the first of the Fire Thieves. But after what happened to him back then, the searchers will probably not be on the lookout for another Fire Run by the old fellow.'

'He lost his nerve,' Luka remembered.

That warnt right of me to mention, Coyote said. *Taint proper to dishonour the great. But since Hercules shot the eagle the Old Boy lives pretty quiet.*

'Or the vulture,' Luka said.

Or the vulture. Warnt none of us there at the time to verify, and the Old Boy, he dont talk so much no more.

'And another good thing about all this rushing about,' Soraya murmured in Luka's ear, 'is that it will allow you to get close to the Bridge, if you rush about too and look like you're searching for yourselves.'

They'll be looking for me an my associates, Coyote said. *Best we part ways. It's fixin to get kindly heated in my vicinity. But look for me to make my run and then you put your best foot forward an make yours.* He loped away without another word.

All at once Luka realised that Nobodaddy had disappeared. One minute he had been there, listening, fidgeting with his panama hat, and then without so much as a *poof*, he was nowhere to be seen. 'What's he up to, I'd very much like to know?' Luka thought. 'I don't feel good about him vanishing like this.' Soraya put a hand on his shoulder. 'You're better off without him,' she said. Then Nuthog the red dragon had her idea, and Luka put Nobodaddy out of his mind.

'Once upon a time our sister Gyara-Jinn helped the King of the Horses escape from Sniffelheim,' said the red dragon, nodding at her golden sibling. 'Yes! The mighty Slippy, that gigantic, white, eight-legged steed – with two legs at each corner, so to speak – had been arbitrarily, unfairly imprisoned there by the Aalim, just as my sisters were until Queen Soraya here set them free by her own powerful magic. The Three Jos had decided there was no place in all of Time for an eight-legged wonder-horse. Just like that – decided it, without any discussion, like tyrants; with no consideration for anyone's feel-ings, Slippy's feelings included. They can be cruel and wanton and wilful when they want to be, even though they pridefully call themselves the Three Inevitable Truths! Anyhow, it was Jinn here who freed Slippy with her dragon-fire – her breath is hotter than mine or Badlo's or Sara's, and proved hot enough to melt the Eternal Ice, which ours did not. In return, the King of the Horses gave her a magnificent gift: the power to Change, just once, whenever the need might be very great, into an exact replica of Slippy himself. No god will dare to search Slippy the King of the Horses as he passes over Vibgyor. We'll strap in each of you – you, Luka, and your dog and bear – between one of the pairs of legs, which leaves one pair of legs for you, Queen Soraya, if you would like . . .'

'No,' Soraya said sadly. 'Even with the Flying Carpet of King Solomon folded away, I'm afraid the presence of the Insultana of Ott will not help you, Luka. I have been too offensive about those cold, stuffy, punishing, implacable, destructive old Jos for too long, and they have no Time for me. It will go worse for you if I'm at your side. I will not enter the Heart of the Heart ever again, that's the truth. I have no wish to end up in Sniffelheim, imprisoned in an Ice Sheet. But I will wait for you and speed you to safety if, that is to say when, you return with blazing Ott Potatoes in that little Ott Pot.'

'You'd do this for me?' Luka said to the golden dragon. 'You'd use up this one-time Change just to help me win through? I don't know how to thank you enough.'

'We owe everything to Queen Soraya,' said Gyara-Jinn. 'That is the person whom you need to thank.'

'Who could have imagined,' Luka told himself ruefully, 'that I, Luka Khalifa, aged only twelve, would be crossing the great bridge Vibgyor, the most beautiful bridge in the entire Magical World, a bridge built entirely of rainbows and brushed by the west wind, gentlest of all the winds, blown softly from the lips of the god Zephyr himself; and yet the only thing I can see and feel is the bristly hair on a giant horse's inner thighs. Who would have thought that out there are some of the greatest names in the history of the Unseen World, the names of the once-worshipped, once-omnipotent Divinities with whom I grew up, about whom I heard each night in my father's endless supply of bedtime stories, the sword Kusanagi, the ex-gods Tonatiuh, Vulcan, Surtr and Bel; and the Bennu bird, and Ra the Supreme; and yet I can't catch even a glimpse of them, or allow them to get the tiniest glimpse of me. Who would have believed that I, Luka, would be entering the Garden of Perfect Perfumes which circles the Lake of Wisdom and is the sweetest-smelling place in all of Existence, and yet the only thing I can smell is horse.'

He could hear noises such as he had never heard in his life: the shriek of a falcon, the hiss of a snake, the roar of a lion, the burning of the sun, all magnified beyond imagining and almost beyond endurance, the war cries of the gods. The Changer Gyara-Jinn in the form of the King of Horses whinnied, neighed, stamped her (or, for the moment, his) eight feet in response, and the intruders concealed between her (or, for the moment, his) legs shook and cringed. Luka didn't like to imagine how Bear and Dog were feeling. Underneath a horse, wedged in between its legs, was no place for a dog, or a bear. There must be a certain loss of pride involved, and he was upset to be the reason for their feelings of shame. He was leading them into great danger, too, he knew that, but he had to close his mind to that thought if he was to stand any chance of doing what needed to be done. '*I am exploiting their love and loyalty*,' he thought. '*It seems there is no such thing as a purely good deed, a completely right action. Even this task, which I took on for the very best of reasons, involves making choices that are not that "good", choices that might even be "wrong".*'

In his mind's eye he saw again the faces of Queen Soraya and the Memory Birds, as they had looked when he said his farewells. Their eyes were moist with tears, and he knew it was because they feared they would never see him again. To this thought, too, he needed to close his mind. He was going to prove them all wrong. If a thing had never been done before, that only meant it was still waiting for the one who could pull it off. '*See how narrow I have become,*' he thought. '*I have turned myself into a single, inevitable thing. I am an arrow speeding towards a target. Nothing must deflect me from my chosen course.*'

Somewhere in the sky up above him were Nuthog, Badlo and Sara, flying in formation in their dragon incarnations. There was no turning back now. The seven of them had entered the inner sanctum of the Aalim with crime in their hearts. The country below them was filled with wonders, but there was no time for sightseeing. All his life, ever since Rashid Khalifa started telling him stories, Luka had wondered about the Torrent of Words that fell to Earth from the Sea of Stories, which was up above the world on its invisible second moon. What would that look like, that waterfall tumbling from space? It must be wonderful to behold. Surely it would splash like an explosion into the Lake of Wisdom? Yet Rashid had always said that the Lake of Wisdom was calm and still, because Wisdom could absorb even the largest Rush of Words without being disturbed. There at the Lake it was always dawn. The long, pale fingers of the First Light rested quietly on the surface of the waters, and the silver sun peeped over the horizon but did not rise. The Aalim who controlled Time had chosen to live at the Beginning of it for ever. Luka could close his eyes and see it all, he could listen and hear his father's voice describing the scene, but now that he was actually there it was very frustrating not to be able to take a look.

And where was Nobodaddy? 'Still Noplace to be seen,' thought Luka, who was surer with every passing minute that the missing phantom was up to no good, wherever he was. 'I will have to face him before the end, I'm sure of that,' he thought, 'and it isn't going to be easy, but if he thinks I'll give up my dad to him without a fight, he's going to be very much surprised.' Then he was struck, as if by a powerful fist, by the worst thought in the world. '*Had Nobodaddy gone because Rashid Khalifa had already . . . already . . . had finally . . . before Luka could save him . . . gone, too? Had the phantom who was absorbing his father vanished because its purpose had been achieved? Was all of this in vain?*' Luka began to tremble at the thought and his eyes grew wet and prickly and grief began to flood over him in great shuddering waves.

But then something happened. Luka became aware of a change within himself. He felt as if something more powerful than his own nature had taken control of him, some will stronger than his own that was refusing to accept the worst. No, Rashid's life was not over. It could not be, therefore it was not. The will-stronger-than-Luka's-own rejected that possibility. Nor would it allow Luka to give up, to flinch in the face of danger or cower in the face of terror. This new force that had gripped him was giving him the strength and courage he would need if he was going to do what needed to be done. It felt like something not-himself, something from *outside*, and yet he also knew that it was coming from within him, that it was his own strength, his own determination, his own refusal of defeat, his own strong will. For this, too, Rashid Khalifa's storytelling, the Shah of Blah's many tales of young heroes finding extra resources within themselves in the face of horrible adversity, had prepared him. 'We don't know the answers to the great questions of who we are and what we are capable of,' Rashid liked to say, 'until the questions are asked. Then and only then do we know if we can answer them, or not.'

And above and beyond Rashid's stories lay the example of Luka's brother Haroun, who had found such an answer in himself, afloat on the Sea of Stories, once upon a time. 'I wish my brother was here to help me,' Luka thought, 'but he isn't, not really, even though Dog the bear is speaking in his voice and trying to take care of me. So I'm going to do what he would have done. I'm not going to lose.'

'*The Aalim are set in their ways and dislike people who try to rock the boat,*' Rashid Khalifa had told the sleepy Luka one night. '*Their view of Time is strict and inflexible: yesterday, then today, then tomorrow, tick, tock, tick. They are like robots marching along to the beat of the disappearing seconds. What Was, Jo-Hua, lives in the Past; What Is, Jo-Hai, simply is right now; and What Will Come, Jo-Aiga, belongs to a place we cannot go. Their Time is a prison, they are the jailers, and the seconds and minutes are its walls.*

'*Dreams are the Aalim's enemies, because in dreams the Laws of*

Time disappear. We know – don't we know, Luka? – that the Aalim's Laws do not tell the truth about Time. The time of our feelings is not the same as the time of the clocks. We know that when we are excited by what we are doing, Time speeds up, and when we are bored, it slows down. We know that at moments of great excitement or anticipation, at wonderful moments, Time can stand still.

'Our dreams are the real truths – our fancies, the knowledge of our hearts. We know that Time is a River, not a clock, and that it can flow the wrong way, so that the world becomes more backward instead of less, and that it can jump sideways, so that everything changes in an instant. We know that the River of Time can loop and twist and carry us back to yesterday or forwards to the day after tomorrow.

'There are places in the world where nothing ever happens, and Time stops moving altogether. There are those of us who go on being seventeen years old all our life, and never grow up. There are others who are miserable old wretches, maybe sixty or seventy years old, from the day they are born.

'We know that when we fall in love, Time ceases to exist, and we also know that Time can repeat itself, so that you can be stuck in one day for the whole of your life.

'We know that Time is not only Itself, but is an aspect of Movement and Space. Imagine two boys, let's say you and young Ratshit, who both wear wristwatches that are perfectly synchronised, and that both keep perfect Time. Now imagine that that lazy rascal Ratshit sits in the same place, let's say right here, for one hundred years, while you run, never resting, all the way to school and back here again, over and over, also for one hundred years. At the end of that century, both your watches would have kept perfect Time, but your watch would be six or seven seconds slower than his.

'There are those of us who learn to live completely in the moment. For such people the Past vanishes and the Future loses meaning. There is only the Present, which means that two of the three Aalim are surplus to requirements. And then there are those of us who are trapped in yesterdays, in the memory of a lost love, or a childhood home, or a dreadful crime. And some people live only for a better tomorrow; for them the Past ceases to exist.

'I've spent my life telling people that this is the truth about Time, and that the Aalim's clocks tell lies. So naturally the Aalim are my mortal enemies, which is just fine, because as a matter of fact I am their deadly foe.'

The Changer Gyara-Jinn stopped galloping, slowed down to a walk, then stopped completely and began to change. The giant eight-legged horse started becoming smaller; its hairy skin vanished and was replaced by a smooth shiny surface; the smell of horse faded away and Luka's nostrils were filled, instead, by the far less palatable odour of the pigpen. Finally the eight legs became four, so that Luka, Bear and Dog slipped out of their bindings and tumbled what was now only a short distance to the admittedly stony ground. Gyara-Jinn's once-in-a-lifetime transformation into the King of Horses had come to an end, and she was a tin sow once again. But Luka wasn't paying any attention to that dramatic Change, because he was staring open-mouthed at the heart-stopping sight he had come so far to see. He was standing at the foot of the vast massif of the Mountain of Knowledge, and just a few feet away, lapping at the Mountain's feet, was the Lake of Wisdom itself, its water clear, pure and transparent in the pale, silvery light of the Dawn of Days, which never brightened into morning. Cool shadows stretched across the water, as always, caressing and smoothing it. It was a ghostly scene, at once haunted and haunting, and it was easy to imagine music in the air, a tinkling crystal melody: the legendary Music of the Spheres that had played when the World was born.

The Shah of Blah's description of the Lake and its inhabitants, which Luka had heard so often that he knew it by heart, proved to be startlingly accurate. Shining schools of little cannyfish could be seen below the surface, as well as the brightly coloured smartipans, and the duller, deep-water shrewds. Flying low over the water's surface were the hunter birds, the large pelican-billed scholarias and the bald, bearded, long-beaked guroos. Long tendrils of the lake-floor plant called sagacity were visible waving in the depths, and Luka recognised the Lake's little groups of islands, too, the Theories with their wild, improbable growths, the tangled forests and ivory towers of the Philosophisles, and the bare Facts. In the distance was what Luka had longed to behold, the Torrent of Words, the miracle of miracles, the grand waterfall that tumbled down from the clouds and linked the World of Magic to the Moon of the Great Story Sea up above.

They had given the hunters the slip and arrived at the notorious South Face of Knowledge without being caught, but looming above Luka was an obstacle far more forbidding than he had imagined, the sheer cliff of the Mountain, a rugged wall of black stone upon which no plant had managed to find a foothold. 'If a plant can't do it, how can I?' Luka wondered in dismay. 'What sort of mountain is this, anyway?'

He knew the answer. It was the Magic Mountain, and it knew how to protect itself. 'Knowledge is both a delight and an explosive minefield; both a liberation and a trap,' Rashid used to say. 'The way to Knowledge shifts and changes as the world changes and shifts. One day it is open and available to all, the next it is closed and guarded. Some people skip up that Mountain as if it were a grassy slope in a park. For others it is an impassable Wall.' Luka scratched the top of his head, just the way his father liked to do. 'I guess I'm one of the others,' he thought, 'because that doesn't look like any grassy slope I've ever seen.' To be blunt, the Mountain looked impossible to climb without serious mountaineering equipment, to say nothing of the proper training, and Luka lacked both. Somewhere above him, at the top of that world of stone, the Fire of Life burned in a temple, and there was no way of knowing where that cave might be, or how to go about finding it. Luka's principal advisers were no longer at his side. Queen Soraya of Ott had not crossed the Rainbow Bridge, and the much less trustworthy (but formidably well informed) Nobodaddy had evidently decided – *for whatever reason, and no not that one!* – to withdraw his support.

'Might I remind you,' said the voice of Nuthog, in gentle tones, 'that you do still have help available, and that that help possesses – may I point out? – *wings*.'

Nuthog, Badlo and Sara were still in dragon-mode, and Jinn quickly dragonised herself as well. 'With four fast dragons at your service you should be able to reach the Fire Temple quickly enough,' Nuthog said. 'Particularly if those four fast dragons happen to know where on the summit the Temple actually is.'

'To know approximately,' said Badlo, rather more modestly.

'We think, anyway,' said Sara, and that didn't sound convincing at all.

'At any rate,' added Jinn, more helpfully, 'before we get going, it would probably be a good idea if you punched . . . *that*.'

That was a silver knob embedded in the stone wall of the South Face. 'It looks like a saving point,' Luka said, 'but why is it silver, not gold?'

'The gold button is in the Temple,' said Nuthog. 'But at least you can save the progress you've made so far. And be careful. From now on, every mistake you make could cost you a hundred lives.'

That was alarming, Luka thought as he punched the silver button. It left almost no room for mistakes. Four hundred and sixty-five lives allowed him four slip-ups, maximum. Besides, while Nuthog's offer of flying him up to his goal was certainly generous, and practical, too, Luka clearly remembered his father's words about the Mountain of Knowledge: 'If you want to reach the summit of the Mountain and discover the Fire of Life, you must make the final ascent alone. The Heights of Knowledge are reached only if you earn the right to do so. You have to put in the hard work. You can't cheat your way to the Top.' He had said something else after that, and Luka remembered thinking that that last bit was the really important part, but he couldn't call it to mind. 'That's the trouble,' he thought, 'with being told all this stuff at night, when you're always dead tired and falling asleep.'

'Thank you very much,' said Luka to Nuthog, 'but I think I'm supposed to solve this riddle and get there by myself. To fly up on your back . . . well, it just wouldn't be right.'

For some reason that idea, *not right*, stuck in his head. The words kept replaying, again and again, as if his thoughts had become stuck like a scratched record, or caught in some sort of loop. *Not right. Not right.* What was a thing if it was not right? Well, yes, *wrong*, that was what most people would say, but it could also be –

'Left,' he said aloud. 'That's the answer. I went right, and fell into the World of Magic. Now maybe if I somehow *go left*, I'll find my way through it.'

Luka remembered his big brother Haroun's many teasing warnings, back home in Kahani, which felt, just at that moment, very far away indeed. *Just be careful not to go down the Left-hand Path.* That's what Haroun had said. 'But I don't like to be teased,' Luka reminded himself, 'and so maybe I should do the opposite of what he said. Yes! Just this once, I'm not going to listen to my brother's advice, because Right-thinking people can never really understand what it is to be on the Left, and that hidden Path is exactly the Path that will get me where I need to go.'

After all, his mother Soraya would be on his side. *Maybe you are correct to believe that the left way round is the right way, and that the rest of us are not right, but wrong.* That's what she had said, and that was more than enough for him.

'I'll go with you,' said Bear the dog loyally.

'I'll go too,' said Dog the bear, not quite as enthusiastically.

And then Luka recalled the really important part of what Rashid Khalifa had told him about the Mountain: '*To climb Mount Knowledge, you have to know who you are.*' Luka, sleepy, bedtime Luka at home far away and long ago, hadn't really understood. 'Doesn't everyone know that?' he had asked. 'I mean, I'm just me, right? And you're you?' Rashid had caressed his hair, which always soothed Luka and made him drowsy. 'People think they're all sorts of things they aren't,' he had said. 'They think they're talented when they're not; they think they're powerful when they're actually just bullies; they think they're good when they're bad. People fool themselves all the time, and they don't know that they're fools.'

'Well, I'm me, anyway; that's all there is to it,' Luka had said, just as he had fallen asleep.

'There he is! There's the Fire Thief! There he goes!'

'It's Coyote! He has a burning brand between his teeth!'

'Look at him go! See him dodge and swerve!'

'Stop him! – Oh, they'll never catch him! – Stop that Coyote! – Oh, he's like hairy lightning! – Stop, thief! Stop the Fire Thief!'

Luka snapped out of his reverie and saw Coyote emerging from the shadows at the foot of Mount Knowledge with fire blazing from his mouth, and streaking round the Mountain towards its far side, running faster than Luka would have believed it was possible for a coyote to run. He was heading across stony ground in the opposite direction from the Rainbow Bridge, leading his pursuers deliberately away from Luka's probable escape route and into the Wild Waste that lay beyond the Lake. This was an area of semi-desert, more properly known as the Waste of Time, a large expanse of arid land which had been overrun, long ago, by a virulent outbreak of Slackerweed. This rapidly spreading weed, previously unknown in the Magic World, had first choked and destroyed all other plant life – except for a few of the hardiest cacti – and then bizarrely self-destructed, as if it had no idea what to do with itself, and no real desire to find out. It just lay apathetically on the ground until it withered away, leaving behind this yellow wilderness dotted with the skulls of long-dead creatures. Snakes slithered out from under rocks and buzzards wheeled overhead, and it was well known that the gods, accustomed as they were to luxury and opulence, were not fond of entering this zone, where, Rashid Khalifa had told Luka, the air moved slowly, the breeze blew without any real sense of direction, and there was something in that wind that induced carelessness, laziness and sleep. Only a few of the guardian deities who had answered the Fire Alarm had been willing to follow Coyote into the Waste, and their pursuit of the fleeing animal seemed slower, groggier and less purposeful than it should have been. Coyote, however, seemed immune to the infectious lethargy in the air. 'The Wild Waste is his natural habitat,' Luka thought. 'He'll give those gods a good run for their money there.' And positioned at intervals along the route Coyote had chosen were the Lion, the Big Bear, the Little Bear, the Wolf, the Squirrel and the Frog. Would the Waste of Time affect them, Luka wondered, or had Coyote discovered an antidote? It wasn't important. The decoy relay had begun.

He heard Coyote's voice in his head, saying, *Put your best foot forward an make your glory run.* And all around him were excited dragons and a barking dog and a roaring bear, and Nuthog was saying, 'It's now or never, young Luka, and if you can't find the way Left, as you say, then you'd best let us fly you up there and take your chances. Move! This is the moment of Truth!'

'Who are those monsters chasing Coyote?' Luka needed to

know. 'If you don't act fast,' Nuthog harrumphed, panicked, 'they'll be chasing you instead, soon enough. Saturn's out there, as savage and violent as any immortal. He eats children, by the way. He's done it before, with his own. And the bearded fellow with the snake wound around him is Zurvan, the Persian time god – you don't want that snake to get within snapping distance, let me tell you! There goes the Dagda, look, that wild Irish fellow with the enormous club! And Xiuhtecuhtli too, though he usually only roams about at night. And even Ling-pao T'ien-tsun – they got him out of the Gossamer Library for once! Looks like they really want to stop the Fire Thief, and when they find out that the fire in Coyote's mouth is a fake – that it's just fire, and not the Fire of Life – then they'll know he was only a decoy, and they'll come after the real Fire Thief in all their fury. So if you know how to climb up this Mountain under your own steam, it would be a good idea to get on with it.'

To decide to do a thing was decidedly not the same thing as actually doing the thing, Luka quickly understood. He really had no idea of exactly how he was supposed to take the little tumble to the left that would shift him into the Widdershins Dimension in which the whole world, including the World of Magic, would morph into Planet Wrongway, the left-handers' home, the southpaw variation of Planet Earth. He tried falling, jumping and rolling to the left; he attempted to trip over his own feet; he asked Bear and Dog to knock him over; and finally, closing his eyes, he tried to feel the Left World pushing at his left shoulder, so that, by pushing back, he could fall through the invisible frontier and get to where he needed to be. None of it worked. His many falls left him considerably the worse for wear, bruised of shoulder and of hip, and with a battered and scratched left leg.

'It beats me,' he admitted, almost in despair.

'The thing about the Left-Hand Path,' said Nuthog gently, 'is that you have to believe it's going to be there.'

Just then a triumphant blast of the Fire Alarm announced the capture of the Fire Thief, followed by two blasts of renewed anguish that announced the hunt was still on. Nuthog whizzed off to investigate as soon as she heard the first blast, and returned to report that after the decoy fire had been passed from Coyote to Lion, and then all the way down the old relay team until it reached Frog, that doughty amphibian had swallowed it and dived into the Circular Sea; whereupon the enraged Worm Bottomfeeder had ended the *carrera de distracción* by swallowing Frog in a single greedy gulp. Four seconds later, Bottomfeeder spat the saliva-covered Frog out again, and roared with all its might to announce to the entire Magical World that this particular Fire Thief was a Common Fraud.

'They're all coming this way now,' Nuthog panted, 'and, to be frank, they're mad as hell, so if you won't let us fly you away from here, then at least run. Run for your life.'

'Yes, I probably should start running,' Luka thought. 'After all, I was running before, when I stumbled the first time and took that magical step to the right.' It was hard to be certain of the laws of Magical Physics; ordinary physics was difficult enough. But what was it Rashid had said? '*Time is not only Itself, but is an aspect of Movement and Space.*' That was the point, wasn't it? 'So, umm, errr,' Luka thought, 'if T is affected by M and S, then, ahhh, therefore, it follows – doesn't it? – that S, which is to say Space, including the Space between the Right-Handed and the Left-Handed Dimensions, must – probably, right? – be an aspect of T and M, i.e. Time and Movement. Or, urrgghh, to put it in English, it makes a difference how long it takes you to make your move, or, in other words, how fast you run.'

The ground began to tremble. 'Is it an earthquake?' Luka cried. 'No,' said Nuthog sadly. 'It's much worse than that. It's the sound of several hundred angry gods moving at speed. It will take a lot more than four dragons to stop that crowd.'

Dog the bear stepped forward with sudden resolution. 'You go,' he said to Luka. 'Go this minute. Take off, *bhag jao*, amscray, vamoose. Go and do the deed. Bear and I can hold them up for quite a while.'

'How?' asked Nuthog sceptically.

'By doing what we do best,' said Dog the bear. 'Are you ready, Bear?'

'Ready,' said Bear the dog.

Luka knew there was no time to discuss the matter. He turned to his left, tilted his left shoulder down a bit, put his left foot forward, and set off at a gallop, as if his life depended upon it. Which, in point of fact, it did.

He ran without looking back. He heard the noise behind him, already loud, getting closer, growing much louder and becoming deafening, like the sound of a thousand jet engines roaring next to his eardrums; he felt the ground beneath his feet, which had already been trembling, begin to shake as if it had been seized by an uncontrollable terror; he saw the sky above him darken, and white lightning begin to stab through the black clouds. 'Okay, so they can put on a show, these gods,' he told himself, to keep his courage up, 'but remember, they aren't gods of anywhere or anyone any more. They're just circus animals, or caged creatures in a zoo.' But a less confident voice whispered into his right ear, 'That may be so, but even in a zoo you shouldn't jump into the middle of the lions' den.' He shook this thought off, put his head down and sprinted harder. Nuthog's advice was the only thing in his head. *The thing about the Left-Hand Path is that you have to believe it's going to be there.* Then all at once the noise seemed to stop, the earth no longer shook, he felt as if he were floating at high speed rather than running, and that was when he saw the abyss.

'Behind the Mountain of Knowledge,' Rashid Khalifa used to say, 'if you are very unlucky, you will find the Bottomless Pit known as the Abysm of Time. And that, by the by, is a rhyme. You pronounce it *abime* and it rhymes with *rhyme*, which also rhymes with *time*. But if you fall into that rhyming Abysm it isn't rhyme that you'll have on your mind.'

Meanwhile, the thundering herd of ex-gods arrived at Mount Knowledge, and found two of the brightest stars of the Great Rings of Fire, the defunct circus of Captain Aag, waiting for them as calmly as the experienced artistes they were, and gesturing courteously to their outside audience to settle down. Bear the singing dog and Dog the dancing bear had taken up their starting positions, along with their backing singers, the Changers, a quartet of giant metallic sows. The sight was unusual enough to stop the discarded deities in their tracks. Ra the Supreme held up his hand and all the ranks of all the former gods, Egyptian, Assyrian, Norse, Greek, Roman, Aztec, Inca and the rest, came clattering to a clumsy halt, full of screeches, collisions and oaths. The Cyclopes accidentally elbowed one another in the eye, the fire gods' burning swords singed the hair of the treasure-nymphs, a basilisk glared at a griffin and accidentally turned it to stone. The beauty goddesses – Aphrodite, cow-eared Hathor and the rest – complained loudest. It appeared that the lower-ranked supernatural entities were taking advantage of the crowd of immortals to squeeze the Beauties' bottoms, accidentally-on-purpose. Also, why exactly were minotaurs stepping on the Lovely Ladies' feet? And, no, the Beauties absolutely did *not* appreciate snake-headed deities from rival mythological traditions looking up their togas. A little space, please, they demanded, a little respect. And shh, by the way, they hissed. There were performers here, and they were ready to begin.

'𓂀𓆓𓊃𓆄,' said Ra, '◆𓈖𓏏◆ 𓈗𓆓𓂋 𓃸𓅓◆◆𓅓𓏤 𓃸𓅓 𓎼𓊃𓊃𓂋𓄿.'

'What on earth was *that*?' asked Bear the dog.

'He's speaking Hieroglyph,' said Nuthog, 'and what he says is, "Okay, this had better be good."'

'Start dancing,' murmured Bear the dog to Dog the bear. 'And dance as you've never danced before.'

'And you start singing,' growled Dog the bear to Bear the dog. 'Sing as if your life depended upon it.'

'Which, in point of fact, it does,' chorused Nuthog, Sara, Badlo and Jinn. 'And ours too, by the way,' Nuthog added. 'No pressure, though. Break a leg.'

So Dog the bear began to dance, first a soft-shoe shuffle, then a rhythm tap, and then the African Gumboot Dance. Once he had warmed up, he went into the Broadway Style and at last his show-stopping speciality, the Caribbean Juba, the most energetic tap dance of them all. The audience went crazy. He had them right where he wanted them; as his feet tapped, so did the feet of the ex-gods; as his hands clapped, so the junked deities clapped along; and when he twirled the Juba Twirl, well, those ancient relics discovered they could still get down and boogie! Ra the Supreme clapped right along with everyone else. '⬚□◆ ○◐&♏ ○◹ □◐■◆◆ ◆◐■◆ ◆□ ♑♏◆ ◆□ ◐■♎ ♌◐■♍♏☒,' he roared, and Gyara-Jinn translated, 'He says, "You make my pants want to get up and dance."' Dog the bear shook his head in wonder. 'But he isn't wearing any pants,' he pointed out. 'Just that little loincloth sort of thing which doesn't exactly hide very much,' agreed Bear the dog, 'but let's not argue.'

'Your turn now,' said Dog the bear to Bear the dog, and the dog murmured back, 'Let's try a little flat-out flattery. After all, it's been a while since anyone worshipped these folks properly.' Then he cleared his throat and burst into howlful melody, singing a series of honeyed odes to the gods of Babylon, Egypt, Asgard, Greece and Rome, improvised from less specifically reverential tunes: 'When I Wish upon Ishtar', 'It's a Beautiful Frey', 'Long-winded Adulation Goes to Memphis on the Nile', and so on. The show seemed to go well, and as he launched into his big finish, the metal sows oohed and clanged behind him.

'*You're dee-vine,*' sang Bear the dog, and the Clangers chorused, '*Ooh (clang), ooh (clang), ooh (clang).*'

'*You're Level Nine,*' sang Bear the dog. '*Ooh (clang), ooh (clang), ooh (clang).*'

'You gorgeous gods of mine,
I really wanna praise you!
Really am amazed by you!
Really wanna praise you now
Cause you look so fine, my gods . . .'

'Ooh (clang), ooh (clang), ooh (clang),'

'My sweet gods . . .'

'Ooh (clang), ooh (clang), ooh (clang).'

'O, my gods —'

Bear was interrupted by an angry roar and a golden blaze of light. Ra the Supreme broke the spell of the music, rose into the sky, glowing furiously, and shot like a bullet towards the summit of Mount Knowledge. All the other ex-gods soared after him, looking like the grandest fireworks display in world history. Bear the dog looked disconsolate. 'I lost my audience,' he said sadly. Dog the bear comforted him. 'It wasn't you. Something just happened up there,' he said. 'Maybe it was something good. Let's hope we bought young Luka enough time.'

An enormous white horse with eight legs galloped towards them, snorting angrily. 'Let's go and see if you did, shall we?' he said. 'By which I mean, you're both under arrest.' This was the real Slippy, King of the Horses, and he didn't look at all pleased to see them. 'As for you and your sisters,' he said to Gyara-Jinn and the other Changers, 'you should consider yourselves seized as well. We'll decide what to do about you later, but treason, may I remind you, is not a minor offence.'

When Luka saw the rhyming Abysm of Time ahead of him he didn't slow down, because now, at last, he could feel the ghostly pressure on his left shoulder that told him the Left-Hand Dimension was *right there, right beside him*, so he ran even faster, and then, at the very edge of the Abysm, he hurled himself to the left . . .

. . . and fell into the Bottomless Pit, and, as he plummeted through the blackness, flew apart into a million shiny fragments. When he came to his senses, his life-counter had subtracted one hundred lives, and he was running at the Abysm again; and again throwing himself left at that area of soft pressure; and again toppling into blackness and disintegrating.

And the third time, the same thing happened *again*. This time, when the shiny fragments of himself re-formed, and he saw that a total of three hundred lives had evaporated in just these few instants, leaving him with only 165, he lost his temper. 'That's pathetic, Luka Khalifa, to be honest with you,' he scolded himself. 'If you can't be serious now, after coming so far, then you deserve the Final Permination you are about to receive.'

Just then a red squirrel ran across his path from right to left, at the very edge of the Abysm, and simply disappeared into thin air. 'Oh, my goodness,' Luka thought, 'I don't even know if there are such things as left-handed – left-footed? – squirrels, but if there are, then this was surely one of them, and it's amazing how easily it hopped across onto the Left-Hand path, without even trying. Obviously when you really and truly believe it's there you can scurry across onto it without the slightest difficulty, whenever you feel the urge.' Whereupon, following the squirrel's example, Luka Khalifa simply turned to the left and took a step, and, without even needing to stumble, stepped into the left-handed version of the Magic World . . .

. . . *in which the Mountain was completely different!* As a matter of fact, it was no longer a Mountain at all, but a low green hill dotted with oaks and elms and chinar trees and stands of poplars, and flower bushes around which honeybees buzzed, hummingbirds hummed and larks warbled melodiously, while crested orănge hoopoes strutted like princes on the grass; and there was a pretty path curling around it to the left, a path which looked like it might take Luka all the way to the top.

'I always knew the Left-Hand World would be much easier for me to handle than the Right-Hand one, if I could just find my way there,' Luka thought happily. 'I bet you that if there was a doorknob anywhere around here, it would turn to the left. It seems that even Knowledge itself is not such a huge, frightening Mountain when the world is arranged to suit us lefties for a change.'

The red squirrel was waiting for him on a low tree stump, nibbling at an acorn. 'Greetings from Queen Soraya,' she said, bowing formally. 'Ratatat's the name. Oh yes. Her Majesty the Insultana thought you might appreciate a little guidance.'

'She certainly has friends everywhere,' Luka marvelled.

'We redheads like to stick together,' said Ratatat, bristling with pleasure. 'And some of us (I don't want to boast, but there it is) are Honorary Otters of long standing – oh yes! – members of the highly confidential Ott List, the Insultana's emergency undercover squadron – sleeper agents, if you will, lurking in our secret Ott Beds and available to the lady twenty-four/seven on her personal Ott Line, just in case she needs to activate us. But, much as I'd like to stop and chat about these Ott Topics, I do believe you might be in something of a hurry. So,' she went on quickly, noticing that Luka had opened his mouth to reply, and obliging him to shut it again, 'let's Ott-foot it up this so-called Mountain while we can.'

Luka almost skipped up that hill, so great was his determination and joy. He had Jumped to the Left, from a Mountain of Difficulty to a Hill of Ease, and the Fire of Life lay within his grasp. Soon he would be rushing home as fast as he could go, to pour the Fire into his father's mouth, and then Rashid Khalifa would surely Awake, and there would be new stories told, and Soraya his mother would sing – 'You do know,' said Ratatat the squirrel, 'that there will be guards?'

'Guards?' Luka stopped dead in his tracks and almost shrieked the word, because somehow he hadn't been expecting to encounter any further obstacles – not here in the Left-Hand Dimension, surely not! Happiness drained from him like blood from a wound.

'You wouldn't expect the Fire of Life to be left unguarded, would you?' said Ratatat sternly, as if lecturing a slightly dim-witted student.

'Are there Fire Gods in this Magic World, too?' asked Luka, and then felt so foolish he actually blushed. 'Well, yes, I suppose there must be – but aren't they all somewhere else right now, guarding the Rainbow Bridge or searching for . . . well, for me, I suppose?'

'As well as Fire Gods,' said Ratatat, 'there are Fire Guards. Oh yes.'

Nowadays, the squirrel explained, the job of guarding the Fire of Life had been given to the most powerful Guard Spirits from all the world's dead religions, aka mythologies. Spotted Kerberos, the fifty-headed dog of Greece and the former gatekeeper of the Underworld; Anzu, the Sumerian demon with the face and paws of a lion and an eagle's claws and wings; the decapitated but still living head of the Nordic giant Mimir, which had been guarding the Fire for so long that it had grown into, and become part of, Mount Knowledge itself; Fafnir the superdragon, as big as the four Changers combined and a hundred times as powerful; and Argus Panoptes, the cowherd with the hundred eyes, who saw everything and missed nothing, were the five appointed guardians, each of them more ferocious than the last.

'Ah,' said Luka, feeling cross with himself. 'Yes, I should have expected that. So, as you know everything, can you tell me how am I supposed to get around that little lot?'

'Cunning,' said Ratatat. 'Do you have that? Because a good supply of that is what is recommended. Hermes, for example, tricked Argus once by cunningly singing him lullabies until all his hundred eyes closed and he fell asleep. Oh yes. To steal the Fire of Life, you'll need to be the cunning, devious, sneaky, tricky, weirdly twisted type. Is that, by any chance, the type of type you are?'

'No,' said Luka disconsolately, and sat down on the grassy slope. 'I'm sorry to say that I'm not.'

As he spoke the sky darkened; storm clouds, black and lightning-lit, thickened overhead. '⟨᷁ᚹ⟩,' said a terrifying voice emanating from the heart of the clouds, '⟨᷁ᚹ⟩.'

'"In that case,"' little Ratatat translated through teeth that were chattering with fear, '"you might find this last step a trifle tough."'

As the gods rose like a swarm of hornets towards the summit of Mount Knowledge, the Fire Alarm sounded the all-clear, announcing the capture of the Fire Thief to the whole Heart of Magic. Bear the dog and Dog the bear, who were being carried up to the top on the Horse King's back, heard the triumphant notes of the siren and were plunged into gloom. Nuthog and her sisters were flying alongside them with their tails very much between their legs. 'The jig is up, I'm sorry to say,' Nuthog told Bear and Dog, confirming their fears. 'It's time to pay the piper.'

At that instant the entire swarm of gods swerved sharply to the left – and, to Bear and Dog's amazement, actually tore through the blue sky itself, as if it were made of paper, and charged through into another sky, which was full of storm clouds. The Horse King and his prisoners followed the swarm through the gigantic rip into the Left-Hand World, and Bear and Dog saw for the first time the transformed version of Mount Knowledge, which they both immediately thought to be the loveliest of green hills, even though the sky was dark and menacing, and the moment so forlorn. At the summit of Knowledge was a flower-strewn meadow crowned by a fine, spreading ash tree. In spite of the tree's beauty, however, its name was the Tree of Terror, and under its boughs stood Luka Khalifa with a red squirrel on his shoulder and the Ott Pot hanging from his neck, guarded by his captor, Anzu the Sumerian thunder demon with his lion's head and eagle's body, who looked as if he was only just managing to restrain himself from ripping the boy to bits with his enormous claws. The rest of the Fire Guards – many-headed Kerberos, Mimir the head without a body, Fafnir the superdragon and Argus Panoptes of the hundred eyes – were also angrily at hand. And beside the great tree was a small, slender-columned marble temple, scarcely larger than a humble garden shed. Inside the Temple was a light that glowed with an almost shocking intensity, filling the air around the Temple with warmth, radiance and a crackle of energy, even in the thunderous mood of that time of failure, captivity and imminent judgement; and above the pillared entrance to the Temple stood a golden ball, the Saving Point at this impossible Level's End. 'That's the glow of Fire of Life,' Dog the bear growled quietly to Bear the dog. 'What a simple home it has, at the end of such a grand journey; and how close we came, and how sad that we didn't –' Bear the dog interrupted sharply: 'Don't say that,' he barked. 'This isn't over.' But in his heart he believed it was.

The trial began. '◆❉☜☞◆✐' roared Ra the Supreme, who seemed to have taken charge of events.

'*Maat!*' the crowd of gods roared back – which is to say roared, or shouted, or chirped, or hissed, depending on the god in question.

'◆❉☜☞◆ ⌘☞• ♌♏♍■ ♎✠•□◆□◆♏♎ ☜■♎ ○◆•◆ ♌♏ □♏•◆□□♏♎✐' shouted Ra.

'*Maat has been disrupted and must be restored,*' echoed the divine mob.

'⟨glyphs⟩' Ra bellowed.

Therefore let Maat be done.

'What's Maat?' Luka asked Ratatat the squirrel.

'Ahem,' said Ratatat, raising her eyebrows and twitching her whiskers professorially. 'It is a reference to the divine music of the Universe – oh yes! – and the structure of the World, and the nature of Time, the most basic of all Forces, which to interfere with is a crime –'

'In short?' Luka requested.

'Oh,' said Ratatat, looking a little disappointed. 'Well, then, in brief, Ra means that order has been disturbed, and justice must be done.'

Luka discovered all at once that he was feeling extremely annoyed. How dare this posse of has-beens judge him? Who were they to tell him he should not try to save his father's life? This was the moment at which he saw his companions arriving on the scene, and the sight of his beloved dog and bear and the four loyal Changers under arrest increased his irritation. These supernatural pensioners had some nerve, he thought. He would have to show them what was what.

'⟨glyphs⟩' cried Ra the Supreme, '⟨glyphs⟩ ⟨glyphs⟩'

'Do I have to translate all that?' said Ratatat reluctantly.

'Yes,' Luka insisted.

'Fortunately for you,' said Ratatat, sighing a little, 'I have an excellent memory, and an obliging nature as well. You won't like it, though. "Once and for all,"' she began, '"members of the Real World must be shown that they are not permitted the use of the Fire of Life. It cannot revive the Dead, for they have entered the Book of the Dead and are no longer Beings, but only Words. But to the Dying it gives new life, and in the healthy it can induce great longevity, even immortality, which belongs to the gods alone. The Fire of Life must not cross the boundary and enter the Real World, and yet here is a Fire Thief who plans precisely to take it across that forbidden frontier. An example must be made."'

'Oh, is that so?' said Luka. A fire of his own making had risen in his breast, and blazed through his eyes. The strange inner force that had gripped him after Nobodaddy's disappearance rose up again and gave him the strength he needed. 'As it happens,' he realised, 'I know exactly what to say.' Then he called out so loudly to the assembled ex-gods that they stopped roaring and hissing and chirping and whinnying and making all the other weird noises they habitually made, and fell silent, and listened.

'It's my turn to speak now,' Luka hollered at the assembled Supernatural Beings, 'and, believe you me, I have a lot to say about all this poppycock, and you had better listen closely, and listen well, because your future depends upon it as much as mine does. You see, I know something you don't know about this World of Magic . . . *it isn't your World!* It doesn't even belong to the Aalim, whoever they are, wherever they are lurking right now. *This is my father's World.* I'm sure there are other Magic Worlds dreamed up by other people, Wonderlands and Narnias and Middle-earths and whatnot – and I don't know, maybe there are some such Worlds that dreamed themselves up, I suppose that's possible, and I won't argue with you if you say it is – but this one, gods and goddesses, ogres and bats, monsters and slimy things, is the World of Rashid Khalifa, the well-known Ocean of Notions, the fabulous Shah of Blah. From start to finish; Level One to Level Nine and back again; lock, stock and barrel; from soup to nuts, it's his.

'He put it together this way, he gave it shape and laws, and he brought all of you here to populate it, because he has learned about you, thought about you, and even dreamed about you all his life. The reason this World is the way it is, is because, Right-Handed or Left-Handed, Nobody's World or the World of Nonsense, this is the World inside his head! And I know about it – probably that's why I was able to stumble to the right and step to the left and get here – because I've been hearing about it every day of my life, as bedtime stories and breakfast sagas and dinner-table yarns, and as tall tales told to audiences all over the city of Kahani and the country of Alifbay, and also as little secrets he whispered into my ears, just for me. So in a way it's now my World, too. And the plain truth is that if I don't get the Fire of Life to him before it's too late, he isn't the only one who will come to an end. Everything here will vanish, too; I don't know what will become of you all exactly but, at the very least, you won't have this comfortable World to live in any more, this place where you can go on pretending you matter when actually nobody gives a hoot. And in the worst-case scenario you will disappear completely – *poof* – as if you had never been, because let's be frank, how many people other than Rashid Khalifa are really bothering to keep your story going nowadays? How many people know any more about the Salamander that lives in Fire, or the Squonk that is so sad about being ugly that it actually dissolves into tears?

'Wake up and smell the coffee, old-timers! You're extinct! You're deceased! As gods and wonderful creatures, you have ceased to be! You say the Fire of Life mustn't cross into the Real World? I'm telling you that if it doesn't reach one particular member of the Real World double-quick, you're done for. Your golden eggs have been fried, and your magic goose is cooked.'

'Wow,' Ratatat the squirrel whispered into his ear. 'You've certainly got their attention now.'

The entire army of discarded divinities had been shocked into amazed silence. Luka under the Tree of Terror knew that he mustn't let anything break the spell. And besides, he had plenty more to say.

'Shall I tell you who you are now?' he shouted. 'Well, first I'll go on reminding you who you aren't. You aren't really the gods of anywhere or anyone any more. You no longer have the power of life and death and salvation and damnation. You can't turn into bulls and capture Earth girls, or interfere in wars, or play any of those other games you used to play. Look at you! Instead of real Powers, you have Beauty Contests. It's a bit on the feeble side, to be honest with you. Listen to me: it's only through Stories that you can get out into the Real World and have some sort of power again. When your story is well told, people believe in you; not in the way they used to believe, not in a worshipping way, but in the way people believe in stories – happily, excitedly, wishing they wouldn't end. You want Immortality? It's only my father, and people like him, who can give it to you now. My father can make people forget that they forgot all about you, and start adoring you all over again and being interested in what you've been getting up to and wishing that you wouldn't end. And you're trying to stop me? You should be begging me to finish the work I came here to do. You should be helping me. You should be putting the Fire into my Ott Pot, making sure it lights up my Ott Potatoes, and then escorting me all the way home. Who am I? I'm Luka Khalifa. I'm the only chance you've got.'

It was the greatest speech of his life as a performer, delivered on the most important stage on which he had ever set foot; and he had used every ounce of skill and passion in his body, that was true – but had he carried his audience with him? 'Maybe so,' he thought worriedly, 'and maybe no.'

Bear the dog and Dog the bear, still on the Horse King's back, were shouting out supportively, yelling, 'That's telling them!' and so on, but the silence of the gods grew so dense, so oppressive, that in the end even Bear held his tongue. That awful silence went on thickening, like a fog, and the dark skies grew darker until the only light Luka could see was the glow from the Fire Temple, and in that flickering radiance he saw the slow movements of giant shadows all around him, shadows that looked like they were closing in on the Tree of Terror and the boy who stood captive beneath it with a Sumerian thunder demon as his guard. Closer and closer the shadows came, forming themselves into a single giant fist that was closing around Luka, and would, any minute now, squeeze the life out of him like water from a sponge. 'This is it, then,' he thought. 'My speech didn't work, they didn't buy it, and so here's an end to it all.' He wished he could hug his dog and his bear once more. He wished the people he loved were there to hold his hand. He wished he could wish himself out of this jam. He wished . . .

The Mountain of Knowledge began to shake violently, as if some invisible colossus were jumping up and down on its slopes. The trunk of the Tree of Terror cracked from top to bottom, and the Tree fell in ruins to the ground, its crashing branches narrowly missing Luka and the thunder demon. One falling branch struck Mimir the Head, and he unleashed an injured yelp. From among the ranks of the gods and monsters there were many more cries, of anguish, bewilderment and fear. Then came the most terrifying events of all. There were instants, very brief, fractions of seconds, when *everything completely disappeared*, and Luka, Bear and Dog – the three visitors from the Real World – remained suspended in an appalling, colourless, sound-less, motionless, lawless, everything-less *absence*. Then the Magic World came back again, but a horrible realisation began to dawn on everyone and everything there: the World of Magic was in trouble. Its deepest foundations were shaking, its geography was becoming uncertain, its very existence had begun to be an intermittent, on–off affair. What if the 'off' moments started getting longer? What if they began to last longer than the 'on' ones? What if the 'on' moments, the periods of the World's exis-tence, diminished to split seconds, or even vanished entirely? What if everything the Fire Thief had just told them was the naked truth, in which they had until now refused to believe, clothed as they all were in the tatters of their old divine glory and the remnants of their pride? Was this the bare, unvarnished reality: that their survival was tied to the ebbing life of a sick and dying man? These were the questions plaguing all the inhab-itants of the Magic World, but in Luka's panicked, racing mind there was a simpler, more horrifying query.

Was Rashid Khalifa about to die?

Anzu the thunder demon fell to its knees and began to plead with Luka in a soft, sad, piteous voice, '꧀ꩠ ꩀ, ꩀ: ⟍ ⎩,, ꩠꩠ, ꩀꩠ, ꩠ ꩫ, ꩫ ꩠ ꩫ ꩢ ꩫꩀꩫ ꩫ, ꩫꩠꩀ, W ꩠ ꩫ ꩫ, ꩢ ꩫꩫꩫ ⟍: W ꩠ ꩫ ꩫ, ꩢ... ꩫv⎯.' Ratatat was so scared that her voice shook as she translated the Sumerian. '"Save us, sir! Only, please, sir, we don't want to be just fairy tales. We want to be revered again! We want to be . . . divine."'

'Sir, huh?' Luka thought. 'That's a change of tone if ever I heard one.' Hope surged through his body, fighting against his despair; he rallied all his strength to make one last effort, and said with all the force he could command, 'Take it or leave it, all of you. It's the best offer you're going to get.'

The darkness stopped closing in around him; the wrath of the gods wavered; overcome by their fear, it broke into pieces and dissipated completely, to be replaced by abject terror. The clouds of anger parted, the daylight returned, and everyone could see that the rip in the sky through which the god-swarm had poured had grown ten times as large as before; that there were actually cracks running across the heavens from horizon to horizon; and that the army of mythological figures was itself deteriorating – ageing, cracking, fading, weakening, diminishing and losing the ability to be. Aphrodite, Hathor, Venus and the other Beauty goddesses looked at the wrinkled skin on their hands and arms and shrieked, 'Smash all the mirrors!' And the immense figure of the falcon-headed Egyptian Supreme Deity fell to its knees just like Anzu had, its body beginning to crumble like an ancient monument; and all the other gods followed Ra's lead – or at least those of them who had knees. In a low, respectful, frightened voice, Ra the Supreme said, '⌖♏⌫●● ♦♋&♏ ♓♦📪'

'What did he say?' Luka asked Ratatat, who had started jumping up and down on his shoulder, squeaking loudly.

'He says they'll take it – your offer, that is,' squeaked Ratatat, in a voice that was simultaneously relieved and terrified. 'You can take the Fire now. Hurry! What are you waiting for? Save your father! Save us all! Don't just stand there! Move!'

Shadows rushed across the sky above their heads. 'Well, will you look at that!' said the welcome voice of the Insultana of Ott. 'I thought I was leading my loyal Otter Air Force on a doomed-but-gallant rescue attempt of an incompetent but oddly likeable young fellow, because, in spite of your foolhardiness, in the final analysis I couldn't stand by and leave you to your fate with only my Honorary Otter Ratatat to represent me; but I see – to my considerable surprise, considering what a foolish boy you are – that you have managed pretty well on your own.' There in the newly cloud-free, but also decaying, sky above the Mountain of Knowledge was the entire OAF on its flying carpets, with quantities of rotten vegetables and itching-powder paper planes at the ready, and Queen Soraya at their head aboard *Resham*, the Flying Carpet of King Solomon the Wise, along with Coyote the decoy runner, the Elephant Birds – 'We came too!' they shouted down. 'We don't just want to remember stuff! We want to *do* stuff too!' – and a male stranger of great age and improbable size, who was also completely naked, with a heavily scarred midriff.

Luka didn't have time to reply to anyone, or to ask who the naked stranger was, or even to embrace Bear and Dog, who had jumped off the Horse King's back and rushed to his side. 'I have to get to the Fire,' he cried. 'Every second counts.' Bear the dog reacted at once, and charged at breakneck speed into the Fire Temple, to return a few seconds later with a burning wooden brand between his teeth, ablaze with the brightest, most cheerful, most attractive, most hopeful fire Luka had ever seen; and Dog the bear climbed the columns of the Fire Temple and, with one great paw, hammered the golden ball over the entrance as hard as he could. Luka heard the telltale little *ding*, saw the number in the top right-hand corner of his field of vision click up to 8, grabbed the burning wood from Bear's jaws and plunged it into the Ott Pot, whereupon the little Ott Potatoes began to burn with the same heart-warming, optimistic cheeriness as the stick.

'Let's go!' yelled Luka, hanging the Pot around his neck again. Its warmth felt comforting; and Soraya swooped down to allow Luka, Bear and Dog to leap up onto King Solomon's Carpet. 'No faster mode of transport in the whole Magic World,' she cried. 'Say your farewells and let's be on our way.' Then Nuthog and her sisters and the squirrel Ratatat shouted, 'No time for that! Goodbye! Good luck! Go!' And so they did. Soraya's carpet hurtled back through the rip in the sky. 'You came in from the Right-Hand World, so that's the way you'll have to go back out,' she told him. The rest of the Otter Air Force followed, but the Carpet of King Solomon was flying at its very fastest, and the others were soon left behind.

'Don't you worry,' said Soraya in her most determinedly cheerful voice. 'I'll get you back in time. After all, it turns out that you have our whole World to save as well as your dad.'

8

The Race Against Time

The sky was falling. They were flying through the hole in the sky, and parts of the heavens were dropping off and crashing down on to the Heart of Magic below. Luka (once again wrapped up for warmth in Soraya's charmed blanket) could not feel the wind inside the defensive bubble Soraya had erected around the flying carpet, but he could see its effects on the world below. Whole trees had been uprooted and went flying through the air as if they had been blown off a huge dandelion clock; fierce leather-winged dragons were being tossed hither and yon like children's toys; and the Gossamer Net Heaven, the most fragile area of the Heart of Magic, made up of fifty-five layers of glistening webs, had been torn to shreds. The 'Great Pure Realm', the legendary Library of Ling-pao T'ien-tsun, which had survived for thousands of years in the Gossamer Nets, was no more. Its ancient volumes were borne aloft, their torn pages fluttering like wings. 'The Winds of Change are blowing,' cried the Elephant Drake, and the Elephant Duck mourned, 'Our little knowledge counts for nothing when you compare it to the wisdom that is being destroyed today.' It was almost impossible for Luka to hear what they were saying because there was a screaming in the wind that seemed, well, *alive*. It was Coyote, his hair standing on end, who explained that *the Wind Shriekers are loose, an when they get to shriekin, why the whole of creation is fit to come apart at the seam*. Luka decided he didn't want to ask who or what the Wind Shriekers might be.

Luka, along with Coyote, the Elephant Birds, Bear the dog and Dog the bear, sat tensely near the leading edge of the flying carpet, watching the turbulent World flash past. Behind them, at the carpet's centre, Soraya stood with her eyes closed and her arms outstretched, forcing *Resham* to achieve speeds it had never touched before; and behind her, with his hands on her shoulders, lending her his strength, knelt the gigantic old naked man whom Luka had never met. *It's him*, Coyote hissed into Luka's ear. *The Old Boy. First an greatest. Heard bout your run an came out to lend a hand. The Old Boy. After all this time. It's a fine thing, kid. It honours us all.*

They flew out of the Heart of Magic and the Forking Paths were below them, their waters boiling, leaping into the air to form hanging walls of liquid, then falling back again in floods. 'So this is Level Nine,' Luka heard himself saying, and Soraya answered grimly, 'No, this is the End of the World.'

The Inescapable Whirlpool and the El Tiempo time-trap were swirling around faster and faster, sucking material into their mouths with ever greater force, and Soraya had to take the flying carpet dangerously high, sixty-one miles above the Earth's surface, less than a mile from the Kármán Line, but there was still a moment when Soraya had to take the flying carpet dangerously high, sixty-one miles above the Earth's surface, less than a mile from the Kármán Line, but there was still a moment when Soraya had to take the flying carpet dangerously high, sixty-one miles above the Earth's surface, less than a mile from the Kármán Line, but there was still a moment when Soraya had to take the flying carpet dangerously high, sixty-one miles above the Earth's surface, less than a mile from the Kármán Line, but there was still a moment when – They were almost trapped, and then they broke free and flew like a missile from a boy's slingshot in a direction which Soraya was unable to control. The flying carpet was spinning round and round like a coin and its passengers clung to one another for dear life. Luka didn't notice the Great Stagnation below them, and then they were at the Mists of Time. The Mists were in trouble too: large holes and tears had appeared in that formerly impenetrable wall of grey. Inside the Mists the carpet was still spinning and the Memory Birds wept with the fear of Oblivion and Coyote howled and things could have become unbearable if the 'Old Boy', the Titan Prometheus, had not risen to his feet and spoken for the first time, using words of Power. '*Khulo!*' he roared at the swirling fog of nothingness. 'I did not escape the Bird of Zeus to perish in a fog! *Dafa ho!* Begone, foul Curtain, and let us be on our way.' And at once the flying carpet emerged from the Mists, and Luka could see where they were.

It was not a cheerful sight. They had been blown far away from the River. The City of Dreams was below them now, and as Soraya fought to steer the flying carpet in the right direction, Luka could see the towers of the Dream City toppling like card palaces, its homes lying in roofless ruin, and he saw, too, many of the unhoused Dreams, which only flourished behind drawn curtains in comfortable darkness, staggering into the bright streets to collapse and wither in the light. Nightmares galloped blindly down the City's roads, and only a few citizens seemed unaffected; but even these were wandering about vaguely, not paying attention to the chaos around them, as if they lived in worlds of their own. 'Those must be Daydreams,' Luka guessed.

The collapse of the World of Magic terrified him, because it could only mean that Rashid Khalifa's life was sliding down its last slope, and so, while Luka watched in horror the crumbling of the fields and farms of the Land of Lost Childhood, while he saw the smoke rising from the forest fires burning on the Blue Remembered Hills, while he witnessed the collapse of the City of Hope, all he could think was: '*Get me back in time, please don't let me be too late, just get me back in time.*'

Then he saw the Cloud Fortress of Baadal-Garh heading towards them at high speed, its massive fortifications intact, the Cloud upon which it stood boiling and bubbling like a sped-up film of itself, and with a sinking heart he understood that his final battle still lay ahead. His left hand clutched at the Ott Pot hanging round his neck, and its warmth gave him a little strength. He crawled on all fours along the flying carpet until he reached Soraya — it was impossible to walk on that rippling, zooming, wind-tossed rug — and he asked, already knowing the answers, 'Who is in charge of that Fortress? Do they mean us any harm?' Soraya's face and body were filled with tension. 'I wish we hadn't outrun the Otter Air Force,' she said, almost to herself. 'But, anyway, they wouldn't have been much use against this enemy.' Then she turned sadly to Luka and answered him. 'In my heart of hearts I knew this would happen,' she said. 'I didn't know where or how or when, but I knew they would not stand back. It is the Aalim, Luka – the Guardians of the Fire, the Lords of Time. Jo-Hua, Jo-Hai, Jo-Aiga. A harsher Trinity you never will see. And with them, just as I suspected, there is a traitor and a turncoat. Look, there, upon the battlement. That vermilion bush shirt. That battered panama hat. There is the scoundrel, among the ranks of your deadliest foes.'

Yes, it was Nobodaddy, no longer a transparent spectre, but looking as solid as any man. Rage and misery wrestled with each other in Luka's heart, but he fought them both back. This was a situation for calm minds. The Fortress City of Baadal-Garh was upon them, and as it neared, it grew. The Cloud upon which it stood spread around the Flying Carpet of King Solomon the Wise, and as it encircled them so did the Fortress's lengthening walls. They were in a prison in the sky, Luka realised, and even though the air above them was clear he was sure that some unseen barrier would block their way if they attempted to escape. They were the prisoners of Time, and the flying carpet came to a halt right below the battlement where the creature Luka had known as Nobodaddy stood, looking down at them with scorn.

'Look at me,' he said. 'As you see, you are already too late.'

Luka had to fight for self-control then, but he managed to shout back, 'That can't be true, otherwise you'd no longer be around, would you? If you were telling the truth about what happens when your work is done, then you'd have done that opposite-of-the-Bang thing, you'd – whatever you called it – *un-become*, and you told me you didn't want to do that –'

'*Un-Be*,' Nobodaddy corrected him. 'You should know the

terminology by now. Oh, and when I said I didn't want to do that? I lied. Why would any creature not want to do the thing it was created for? If you're born to dance, you dance. If you're born to sing, you don't sit around keeping your mouth shut. And if you come into being in order to eat a man's life, then finishing the job and Un-Being after it's done is the supreme achievement, the absolutely satisfying climax. Yes! A thing of ecstasy.

'It sounds like you're in love with death, to be honest with you,' said Luka, and then understood the meaning of what he'd said.

'Quite,' said Nobodaddy. 'Now you get it. I do confess to a measure of self-love. And that is not a noble quality, I readily concede the point. But, I repeat: *ecstasy*. All the more so in a case like this one. Your father has fought me with all his might, I should tell you. My compliments to him. He clearly feels he has powerful reasons to stay alive, and maybe you are one of those reasons. But I have my hand on his throat now. And you are right: when I said you were too late, I lied again. Look.'

He held up his right hand, and Luka could see that half of the middle finger was missing. 'That's all the life he has left,' said Nobodaddy. 'And while we're talking, he's emptying out, and I am filling up. Who knows? Maybe you'll still be around to witness the great event. You can certainly forget about getting home in time to save him, even if you do have the Fire of Life in that Ott Pot around your neck. Congratulations on getting that far, by the way. Level Eight! Quite an achievement. But now, let's not forget, Time is on my side.'

'You turned out to be a nasty piece of work, and no mistake,' said Luka. 'What a fool I was to be taken in by you.' Nobodaddy laughed a cold laugh. 'Ah, but if you hadn't gone along with me, there would have been none of this fun,' he said. 'You've made the wait so much more enjoyable. I really have to thank you for that.'

'It's all been just a game to you,' Luka shouted, but Nobodaddy wagged the half-finger at him. 'No, no,' he said reprovingly. 'Never *just a game*. It's a matter of life and death.'

Dog the bear stood up on his hind legs and growled, 'I can't stand this fellow any more. Let me at him.' But Nobodaddy was out of Dog's reach up there on his rampart, and there seemed to be no way up. Then, in his deep, deep voice, the Titan spoke, the scarred Old Boy himself. 'Leave him to me,' he said, and got up from his kneeling position behind Soraya; and rose; and rose; and rose. When a Titan grows to his full size the Universe trembles. (The Universe also tries to look away, because nakedness enlarged in this way is much, much bigger than regular-sized nakedness, and harder to ignore.) Long ago, the Old Boy's uncle had risen up like this and destroyed the sky itself. After that the battle of the Greek gods against the Twelve Titans had shaken the earth as the colossi fought and fell. The Old Boy, a veteran and hero of that war, scorning clothes as Greek Heroes and Ancients always had, rose up and grew so big that Soraya had to hurry to enlarge the flying carpet to its maximum size, before they were all pushed off it by the Old Boy's enlarging feet. Luka was pleased to note the look of fear on Nobodaddy's face as the Titan reached out an enormous left hand, grabbed him, and held him fast. 'Let me go,' squealed Nobodaddy – his voice was sounding inhuman now, Luka thought, it was goblinish, demonic, and, at this precise moment, it was shriekingly scared.

'Unhand me,' shrieked Nobodaddy. 'You have no right to do this!'

The Old Boy grinned a grin the size of a stadium. 'Ah, but I have a left,' he said, 'and we left-handers stick together, you know.'

With that, he drew back his hand as far as it would go, with Nobodaddy kicking and squeaking in his grip, and then he hurled that dreadful, deceiving, life-sucking creature far, far away, up into the sky, howling all the way to the edge of the atmosphere and then out beyond the Kármán Line, where the world ended and the blackness of outer space began.

'We're still trapped,' Dog the bear pointed out grouchily, because he felt a little upstaged by the Titan's titanic effort. Then, too loudly, and in too challenging a manner, he added, 'Where are these Aalim, anyway? Let them show themselves, unless they're too scared to face us.'

'Be careful what you wish for,' said Soraya hurriedly, but it was too late.

'*It is not known*,' said Rashid Khalifa, '*if the Aalim have actual physical form. Perhaps they do have bodies, or perhaps they can simply take on bodily shapes when they need to, and at other times they are disembodied entities, spreading out through space – because Time is everywhere, after all; there's nowhere that doesn't have its Yesterdays, that doesn't live in a Today, that doesn't hope for a good Tomorrow. Anyway, the Aalim are known for their extreme reluctance to appear in public, preferring to work in silence and behind the scenes. When they have been glimpsed, they have always been hidden inside hooded cloaks, like monks. Nobody has ever seen their faces, and everyone is afraid of their passing – except for a few particular children . . .'*

'A few particular children,' Luka said aloud, remembering, 'who can defy Time's power just by being born, and make us all young again.' It had been his mother who had said that first, or something very like it – he knew this because she had made a point of telling him so – but soon enough the idea became a part of Rashid's inexhaustible storehouse of tall stories. 'Yes,' he admitted to Luka with a shameless grin, 'I stole that from your ma. Don't forget: if you're going to be a thief, steal the good stuff.'

'Well,' thought Luka the Thief of the Fire of Life, 'I acted on your advice, Dad, and look what I stole, and you see where it's got me now.'

The three hooded figures standing on the battlements of the Cloud Fortress of Baadal-Garh were neither large nor imposing. Their faces were invisible and their arms were crossed, as if they were cradling babies. They said nothing, but they didn't need to. It was plain from the expression on Soraya's face, and from Coyote's cringing whine – *Madre de Dios, if I warnt on a carpet in the sky right now I'd jus make a run for it an take my chances* – and the quivering of the Elephant Birds – 'Okay, maybe we don't want to do stuff after all! Maybe we just want to live, and remember stuff, like we're supposed to!' – that their mere appearance struck terror into the people of the Magic World. Even the grizzled Old Boy, the great Titan himself, was fidgeting nervously. Luka knew that they were all thinking fearfully about Sniffelheim, about being imprisoned for ever in solid blocks of ice. Or possibly they were worrying about liver-eating birds. 'Hmm,' he thought, 'it looks like our Magic Friends aren't going to be much use in this situation. It's up to the Real World team to pull this off somehow.'

Then the Aalim spoke, in unison, three low, unearthly voices whose triple coldness felt steely, like three invincible swords. Even courageous Soraya quailed at the sound. 'I never thought I would be forced to hear the Voices of Time,' she cried, and put her hands over her ears. 'Oh, oh! It's unbearable! I can't stand it!' and she fell to her knees in pain. The other magic beings were similarly distressed and writhed around on the flying carpet in evident agony, except for the Old Boy, whose tolerance for pain was obviously very great after that eternity at the mercy of the liver-munching Bird of Zeus. Dog the bear looked unimpressed, however, and Bear the dog, whose hackles were up, bared his teeth in an angry snarl.

'*You have taken us away from our Handloom,*' the soft sword-voices said. '*We are Weavers, the three of us, and on the Loom of Days we weave the Threads of Time, weaving the whole of Becoming into the fabric of Being, the whole of Knowing into the cloth of the Known, the whole of Doing into the garment of the Done. Now you have taken us from our Loom and things are disorderly. Disorder displeases us. Displeasure displeases us also. Therefore we are doubly displeased.*' And then, after a pause: '*Return what you have stolen and perhaps we will spare your lives.*'

'Look at what's happening around you,' Luka shouted back. 'Can't you see it? The calamity of this whole World? Don't you want to save it? That's what I'm trying to do, and all you have to do is get out of my way and let me get home –'

'*It is of no consequence to us whether this World lives or dies,*' came the reply.

Luka was shocked. 'You don't care?' he asked disbelievingly.

'*Compassion is not our affair,*' the Aalim replied. '*The ages go by heartlessly whether people wish them to do so or not. All things must pass. Only Time itself endures. If this World ends, another will continue. Happiness, friendship, love, suffering, pain are fleeting illusions, like shadows on a wall. The seconds march forward into minutes, the minutes into days, the days into years, unfeelingly. There is no "care". Only this knowledge is Wisdom. This wisdom alone is Knowledge.*'

The seconds were indeed marching forward, and at home in Kahani Rashid Khalifa's life was ebbing away. 'The Aalim are my mortal enemies,' he had said, and so they were. Passion rose up in Luka, and a scream of angry love burst out of him. 'Then I curse you, just as I cursed Captain Aag!' he yelled at the Three Jos. 'He caged his animals, and treated them cruelly, and you're exactly the same, to be honest with you. You think you have everyone in your cage and so you can ignore us and torment us and make us do what you want, and you don't care about anything except yourselves. Well, curse you, all three of you! What are you, anyway? Jo-Hua, the Past has gone and will never return, and if it lives on, it's only in our memories – and the memories of the Elephant Birds, of course – and it's certainly not standing up there on the ramparts of this Cloud Fortress, wearing a stupid hood. As for you, Jo-Hai, the Present hardly exists, even a boy my age knows that. It vanishes into the Past every time I blink an eye, and nothing as, um, *temporary* as that has much power over me. And Jo-Aiga? The Future? Give me a break. The Future is a dream, and nobody knows how it will turn out. The only sure thing is that we – Bear, Dog, my family, my friends and – *we* will make it whatever it is, good or bad, happy or sad, and we certainly don't need you to tell us what it is. Time isn't a trap, you phoneys. It's just the road I'm on, and I'm in a real hurry right now, so get out of my way. Everyone here has been scared of you for too long. May they lose their fear and – and – and put *you* on ice for a change. Stop bothering me now. I – I snap my fingers at you.'

So there it was. He had defied Time's power, just as his mother (and, later, his father) had said he could, and all he had at the end of it was his recently acquired ability to snap his fingers loudly. It wasn't much of a weapon, really. But it was interesting, wasn't it, that the Aalim had been stopped in their tracks by his curse, and that they had put their heads together and were muttering and murmuring – it seemed to Luka – *helplessly*? Was that possible? Might it be that they were powerless against Luka Khalifa's famous Cursing Power? Could it be that they knew that he was one of the Particular Children who would not be the victims of Time? If this was Rashid Khalifa's Magic World, then were the Aalim his creation, too, and therefore subject to his laws? Very deliberately, like a sorcerer casting a spell, Luka lifted his left hand high above his head and snapped his fingers with all his might.

Right on cue, the encircling Cloud Fortress of Baadal-Garh began to shake like cheap theatre scenery, and, as the prisoners on the flying carpet watched in astonishment, large sections of the crenellated walls of that aerial jail began to crack and fall. 'It's under attack from the outside!' Luka yelled, and everyone on the flying carpet began to cheer as the Aalim disappeared from view to face the unexpected assault. 'Who is it?' Soraya asked, gathering her strength and looking extremely embarrassed about her moment of weakness. 'Is it the Otter Air Force? If so, they're on a suicide mission, I'm afraid.' The naked Titan shook his head, and a slow grin spread over his huge face. 'It's not the Otters,' he said. 'The gods are revolting.'

'Well, on the whole we agree about what the gods are like,' said the Elephant Birds, 'but there's no need to be rude.'

'I mean,' said the Old Boy with a sigh, 'that the gods have risen in revolt.'

And so they had. Looking back on these events later in his life, Luka was never sure if the Revolt of the Gods had been provoked by his speech under the Tree of Torment, when he had tried to persuade the forgotten deities that their survival depended on his father's; or if it had been conjured up by his Curse, whose purpose had been to break the stranglehold of the Aalim over the affairs of both Worlds, the Real and the Magical; or if the retired immortals had decided that enough was enough, and Luka and his friends had just been around at the right time to witness the consequences. Whatever the reason, the hornet-swarm of the ex-gods of the Heart of Magic flew through the rip in the sky and descended in wrath upon the Cloud Fortress of Baadal-Garh. Bast the Cat Goddess of Egypt, Hadadu the Akkadian Thunder God, Gong Gong the Flood God of China whose head was so strong that it could crack the Pillar of Heaven, Nyx the Greek Night Goddess, the savage Nordic Fenris Wolf, Quetzalcoatl the Plumed Serpent of Mexico, and assorted Demons, Valkyries, Rakshasas and Goblins could be seen alongside the big fellows – Ra, Zeus, Tlaloc, Odin, Anzu, Vulcan and the rest – burning the Cloud Fortress, hurling tsunamis against its wall, blasting it with lightning, headbutting it, and, in the case of Aphrodite and the other Beauty goddesses, complaining loudly about the Ravages of Time on their complexions, their figures and their hair.

If there had been a force field protecting the Cloud Fortress, the Assault of Magic[1] had been too much for it. And as the collected might of all the former deities demolished the Aalim's stronghold, and a loud, strange, screechy, miaowing sound was heard, Luka shouted at Soraya, 'This is our chance!' and at once the flying carpet rose high into the sky and bore its passengers away at speed.

The getaway wasn't easy. The Aalim were making their last stand; their day was ending, but they still had some loyal servants to call on. Soraya had only just set a course for the Bund, the embankment on the River Silsila where Luka would have to leap back into the Real World, when a squadron of bizarre one-legged birds, the fabled Shang Yang, or Rainbirds of China, assaulted the flying carpet from above. The Shang Yang carried whole rivers in their beaks and poured them over the *Resham* in an attempt to extinguish the Fire burning in the Ott Pot around Luka's neck. The carpet lurched sideways and plunged downwards under the weight of the falling avalanches of water;

[1] Or, to give it its full title, the Overthrow of the Dictatorship of the Aalim by the Inhabitants of the Heart of the Magical World, and Its Replacement by a More Sensible Relationship with Time, Allowing for Dream-time, Lateness, Vagueness, Delays, Reluctances, and the Widespread Dislike of Growing Old.

but then, showing remarkable powers of recovery, it straightened itself out and flew onwards. The assault of the Rainbirds continued; five, six, seven times the floods fell from the sky, and the carpet's passengers fell over, collided with one another, and rolled dangerously near the edges of the carpet. Still the defensive bubble held firm. At last the Shang Yang's water supply ran dry and they flapped bad-temperedly away. 'Yes, it's good to have resisted this attack, but it's not the end of the trouble,' Soraya warned the cheering Luka. 'The Aalim have made one more desperate effort to prevent the Fire of Life from crossing over into the Real World. You heard that dreadful, piteous miaowing sound that filled the air as we left the Cloud Fortress? That was the Aalim playing their final card. I'm sorry to tell you that that noise was the Summons that unleashes the deadly Rain Cats.'

The Rain Cats – for it is time, at last, to speak of catty matters! – started falling from the sky soon enough. They were large Cats, raintigers and rainlions, rainjaguars and raincheetahs, Water Felines of every spot and stripe. They were made of the rain itself, rain enchanted by the Aalim and turned into sabretoothed Wildcats. They fell as cats fall, nimbly, fearlessly, and when they hit the flying carpet's invisible security bubble they dug their claws in and held on. Soon there were Rain Cats all over the bubble, hundreds of them, then thousands, and their claws were long and powerful, and they slashed at the bubble to great and damaging effect. 'I'm afraid they will break through the shield,' cried Soraya, 'and there are too many of them for us to fight.'

'No, there aren't! Come down here, Fraidy Cats! We'll soon

show you what's what!' Bear the dog barked bravely at the clawing, slashing Rain Cats above him, and the Old Boy prepared to grow to his full height again, but Luka knew all of that was just empty bravado. Thousands of feral enchanted felines would surely overpower even the great Titan, and while Bear and Dog (and maybe even Coyote) would fight for all they were worth, and no doubt Soraya had plenty of tricks up her sleeve, there could, in the end, be no victory against such unequal odds. 'Every time I think we've cracked it,' Luka thought, 'there's another impossible obstacle in my way.' He took Soraya's hand and squeezed it. 'I only have one hundred and sixty-five lives left, and I don't think they will be enough to get me through this last test,' he said. 'So if we lose here, I just want to say thank you, because I would never have come half this far without your help.' The Insultana of Ott squeezed his hand back, looked over his shoulder, and burst into a wide smile. 'No need to get sentimental on me just yet, stupid boy,' she said, 'because you're not only making too many enemies, although you do seem to have no shortage of those. Look behind you. You're also acquiring some pretty powerful friends.'

Enormous banks of cloud had piled up behind the Flying Carpet of King Solomon the Wise; but, Soraya pointed out with glee, those were not mere clouds. They were the assembled Wind Gods of the Magic World. 'And their presence here,' she said reassuringly, 'means that the gods are definitely determined to get you home to do what you have to do.'

Now Luka saw the faces of the Wind Gods inside the cloud banks, cloud faces puffing up their cheeks and blowing with all their might. '*Three* Chinese Wind Gods are here,' Soraya said very excitedly, 'Chi Po, Feng-Po-Po and Pan-Gu! And you see that bunch of flying Wind Lions, the Fong-shih-ye from the Kinmen archipelago of Taiwan? The Chinese usually refuse to speak to them, or even to accept that they exist – but here they are, working together! It's really amazing how everyone has united behind you! Fujin from Japan has come, and he *never* goes *anywhere*. Look there, all the American gods, the Iroquois deity Ga-Oh, and Taté of the Sioux, and, see, the ferocious Cherokee Wind Spirit, Oonawieh Unggi, over there! I mean, the Sioux and the Cherokee were never allies, and to join up with the Iroquois Confederacy – oh, my! And even Chup the Wind God of the Chumash tribe from California has stopped sunbathing and shown up; he's usually too laid-back to rustle up much more than a light breeze. And the Africans are here as well – that's Yansan the Yoruba Wind Goddess! And from Central and South America, Ecalchot of the Niquiran Indians, and the Mayan Pauahtuns, and Unáhsinte of the Zuni Indians, and Guabancex from the Caribbean . . . they're so old, that lot, that frankly I thought they had blown themselves out, but it looks like they have plenty of puff left! And fat Fa'atiu the Samoan is over there, and bulgy Buluga of the Andaman Islands is over *there*, and Ara Tiotio the Tornado God of Polynesia, and Paka'a from Hawaii. And Ays the Armenian Wind Demon, and the Vila, the Slav Goddesses, and the Norse winged giant Hraesvelg who makes the winds just by flapping his wings, and the Korean Goddess Yondung Halmoni – she'd be blowing better if she wasn't stuffing her mouth with rice cakes, the greedy creature! – and Mbon from Burma, and Enlil –'

'Stop, please stop,' Luka begged. 'It doesn't matter what

they're called – what they're doing is more than enough.' What they were doing was this: they were blowing away the Rain Cats. With many loud roars and yowls the Rain Cats lost their grip on the bubble around the flying carpet and were sent flying to nowhere, blown head over heels into the depths of the broken sky. A great cry of happiness went up from everyone aboard the *Resham*, and then the Wind Gods really got going, and the carpet began to travel at the most amazing speed. Even Soraya with all her skill could not have made it go half as fast. The Magic World below them and the sky above became a blur. All Luka could see was the carpet itself and the massed Wind Gods behind it, blowing him all the way home. '*Get me back in time*,' he thought fervently once again. '*Please don't let me be too late, just get me back in time.*'

The wind dropped, the carpet landed, the Wind Gods disappeared, and Luka was home: not on the bank of the Silsila as he had expected, but in his very own lane, in front of his very own house, in the very place where he first heard Dog and Bear speak, where he first met Nobodaddy and embarked on his great adventure. The colours of the world were still strange, the sky still too blue, the dirt too brown, the house much pinker and greener than usual; nor was it normal for a flying carpet to be parked here, with a Sultana of the Magic World, a Titan, a Coyote and two Elephant Birds aboard, all of them looking distinctly ill at ease.

'The truth is we don't belong here, at the Frontier,' said Soraya, as Luka, Dog the bear and Bear the dog stepped off *Resham* into the dusty lane. 'So, since you have to go, go quickly, so that we also can be off. Go to that other Soraya who lives in that house, and when you pop that Ott Potato into your father's mouth, don't forget it was the Insultana of Ott who gave it to you; and afterwards, as you grow into a young man, think about that Insultana sometimes, if you don't completely forget.'

'I'll never forget you,' Luka said, 'but please, can I ask you one last question: can I pick up an Ott Potato with my bare hands? And if I put it into my dad's mouth, won't it burn him to bits?'

'The Fire of Life does not wound those it touches,' said Soraya of Ott. 'Rather, it heals wounds. You will not find that glowing vegetable too hot to pick up. Nor will it do your father anything but good. There are six Ott Potatoes in that Pot, by the way,' she concluded, 'one for each of you, if that's what you decide.'

'Goodbye, then,' said Luka, and then he turned to the Old Boy and added, 'And I meant to say, I'm sorry about what happened to Captain Aag, because he was your brother, after all.' The Old Boy shrugged. 'Nothing to be sorry about,' he said. 'I never liked him anyway.' Then, without further ado, the Insultana Soraya raised her arms, and the Flying Carpet of King Solomon the Wise rose into the sky and vanished with only a soft *whoosh* for farewell.

Luka looked at his front door, and saw, standing on the doorstep, glistening in the day's first light, a large golden orb: the Saving Point for the end of Level Nine, the end of the 'game' that hadn't been a game at all but, as Nobodaddy had said, a matter of life and death. 'Come on,' he shouted to Dog and Bear, 'let's go home.' He ran towards the Saving Point and just as he reached it he stumbled, as he had known he would; he managed to kick the point with his left leg as he lurched awkwardly to his right; he heard, for the last time, the tell tale *ding* that confirmed his achievement; he saw all the numbers vanish from his field of vision; he felt oddly giddy for a moment; then he regained his balance, and saw that the golden orb had vanished, and the colours of the world had returned to normal. He understood that he had left the World of Magic behind, and was back where he needed to be. 'And it looks like the same exact time it was when I left,' he marvelled. 'So all of that never happened, except, of course, that it did.' The Ott Pot was still hanging from his neck, and he could feel its warmth on his chest. He took a deep breath and ran indoors and up the stairs as fast as he could run, and Bear the dog and Dog the bear came too.

The sweet smells of home welcomed him back: his mother's perfume, the thousand and one mysteries of the kitchen, the freshness of clean sheets, the accumulated fragrances of everything that had happened between those walls during all the years of his life, and the older, more obscure scents that had hung in the air since before he was born. And at the top of the stairs was his brother Haroun, with a strange expression on his face. 'You've been somewhere, haven't you?' Haroun said. 'You've been up to something. I can see it on your face.' Luka charged past him, saying, 'I don't have time to explain it right now, to be honest with you,' and Haroun turned and ran after him. 'I knew it,' he said. 'You've had your adventure! So come on, out with it! And by the way, what's that hanging from your neck?' Luka ran on without replying, and Bear the dog and Dog the bear pushed their way past Haroun as Luka rushed into his father's bedroom. They had been part of the adventure, too, and they didn't intend to miss the final scene.

Rashid Khalifa lay in his bed, Asleep with his mouth open, just as he had been when Luka had last seen him, and the tubes were still running into his arm, and the monitor by his bedside showed that his heart was still beating, but very, very faintly. He looked happy, though, he still looked happy, as if he were being told a story that he loved. And by his bedside stood Luka's mother Soraya, with her fingers fluttering at her lips, and Luka understood, the moment he ran into the room and saw her, that she was about to kiss her fingertips and then touch Rashid's mouth, because she was saying goodbye.

'What on earth are you doing, running in here like a crazy person?' Soraya cried, and then Bear the dog, Dog the bear and Haroun charged in as well. 'Stop it, all of you,' she demanded. 'What is this? A playground? A circus? What?'

'Please, Mum,' Luka begged, 'there's no time to explain – please just let me do what I have to do.' And without waiting for his mother's reply, he popped an Ott Potato, glowing with the Fire of Life, into his father's open mouth, where, to his amazement, it dissolved instantly. Luka, staring fiercely through his father's lips, saw little tongues of fire dive down into Rashid's insides; and then they were gone, and for an instant nothing happened, and Luka's heart sank. 'Aah,' his mother was complaining, 'what on earth have you done, you silly boy . . .?' But then the scolding words died on her lips because she, and everyone else in the room, saw the colour return to Rashid's face; after which a glow of health spread across his cheeks, almost as if he were blushing with embarrassment; and the monitor by the bedside began to drum out a firm, regular heartbeat.

Rashid's hands began to move. His right hand darted out without warning and started tickling Luka, and Soraya gasped to see it, half with delight at the miracle of it, half with something like fear. 'Stop tickling me, Dad,' Luka said joyfully, and Rashid Khalifa said without opening his eyes, 'I'm not tickling you – Nobody is,' and then he turned over on his side to attack Luka with his left hand as well. 'You are, you are tickling me,' Luka laughed, and Rashid Khalifa, opening his eyes, and grinning widely, said innocently, 'Me? Tickling you? No, no. That's just Nonsense.'

Rashid sat up, stretched, yawned, and gave Luka a funny, inquisitive look. 'I've been having the strangest dream about you,' he said. 'Let me see if I can remember it. You went adventuring in the World of Magic, I think that was it, and the whole place was falling apart. Hmm, and there were Elephant Birds, and Respecto-Rats, and a real, honest-to-goodness Flying Carpet, and then there was the little matter of becoming a Fire Thief and stealing the Fire of Life. You wouldn't by any chance know anything about that dream, young Luka? You wouldn't by some unlikely chance be able to fill in the blanks?'

'Maybe so and maybe no,' said Luka shyly, 'but you should know already, Dad, because, to be honest with you, it felt like you were right there with me all the time, advising me and filling me in, and I'd have been lost without you.'

'That makes two of us, then,' said the Shah of Blah, 'because

I'd be lost right now if it wasn't for your little exploit, that's for sure. Or, your not-so-little exploit. Or, in fact, your supercolossal ultra-exploit. Not that I want you to grow a big head or anything. But the Fire of Life. *Really*. Quite a feat. Hmm, hmm. Ott Potatoes, is it? And could that thing hanging from your neck in fact be an actual Ott Pot?'

'I don't know what you two are talking about,' said Soraya Khalifa contentedly, 'but it's good to hear the old rubbish being spoken in this house again.'

That wasn't the end of the story, however. Just as Luka was relaxing, certain that his job was done at last, he heard an unpleasant bubbling noise welling up from a corner of his father's bedroom and there, to his horror, was a Creature he thought he had seen for the last time when the Old Boy hurled him out into the deeps of space. It wasn't wearing a vermilion bush shirt or a panama hat any more; it was colourless and faceless, because Rashid Khalifa had gone back into himself, and though this vile death-thing was plainly trying to gather itself into some sort of human shape, it succeeded only in looking twisted and hideous and sort of sticky, as if it were made out of glue. 'You dont' get rid of me as easily as that,' it hissed. 'You know why. *Somebody has to die*. I told you at the beginning there was a catch, and that's it. Once I've been called into being, I don't leave until I've swallowed a life. No arguments, okay? Somebody has to die.'

'Go away,' Luka shouted. 'You lost. My father's fine now. Just bubble off to wherever it is you go.'

Rashid, Soraya and Haroun looked at him in amazement. 'Who are you talking to?' Haroun asked. 'There's nothing in that corner, you know.' But Bear the dog and Dog the bear could see the Creature all right, and before Luka could say any more it was Bear who interrupted. 'How about,' he asked the Creature, 'if an immortal being gives up his Immortality?'

'Why is Bear barking like that?' Soraya asked, bewildered. 'I don't understand what's happening.'

'Remember?' Bear asked Luka urgently. '*I am Barak of the It-Barak, a thousand years old and more*? Turned into a dog by a Chinese curse? You didn't like it much when I told you that, because you wanted me to be your dog and nothing else. Well, now that's all I want to be, too. After a thousand years, that's it. To hell with the past! And who wants to live for another thousand years? Enough of all that! I just want to be your dog, Bear.'

'That's too big a sacrifice,' said Luka, overwhelmed by his dog's loyalty and selfless courage. 'I can't ask you to make it.'

'I'm not asking you to ask me,' said Bear the dog.

'That dog is a lot noisier than I recall,' Rashid said. 'Luka, can't you quieten him down?'

'An Immortality,' said the Creature in the corner hungrily. 'Mmm! Yes, yes! To swallow an Immortality! To suck it out of the Immortal and fill up with it, leaving the ex-Immortal behind in mortal form! Oh yes. That would be very sweet indeed.'

'Ahem,' said Dog the bear suddenly. 'There is something I would like to confess.' At that moment, Luka thought, Dog looked sheepish, not bearish at all. 'You know that story I told you – about being a prince who could spin air into gold? And Bulbul Dev the bird-headed ogre, and so on?'

'Of course I remember,' Luka said.

'See, husband, now the bear is growling, and the boy is talking to the bear,' said Soraya helplessly. 'These animals – and your son as well – are really getting to be impossible to control.'

'It wasn't true,' admitted Dog the bear, hanging his head in shame. 'The only thing I spun out of thin air was that yarn, that shaggy-dog story – or shaggy-bear story, maybe I should say. I just thought I ought to have a good story to tell. I thought it was expected of me at the time, especially after Bear here sang that song about himself. I made it up to make myself look good. I shouldn't have done it. I'm sorry.'

'Don't worry,' said Luka. 'This is a storyteller's house. You should know what it's like by now. Everybody here makes up stories all the time.'

'That's settled, then,' said Bear the dog. 'Only one of us has an immortal life to give up, and that one is me.' And without waiting for any further discussion he ran to the corner where the Creature was crouching, and leapt; and Luka saw the Creature open a ghastly sort-of-mouth impossibly wide, and he saw Bear being swallowed up by that mouth; and then Bear was ejected again, looking the same, only different, and the Creature had become Bear-shaped too: No-Bear, instead of Nobodaddy. 'Ohh,' cried the Creature, 'Ohh, ecstasy, ecstasy!' And there was a sort of backwards flash, as if light were being sucked into a point instead of exploding out from a point, and the Bear-Creature imploded, *whoommpppffff*, and then it wasn't there any more.

'Woof,' said Bear the dog, wagging his tail.

'What do you mean, "woof"?' Luka demanded. 'Cat got your tongue?'

'Growl,' said Dog the bear.

'Oh,' said Luka, understanding. 'The magic part really is over now, isn't it? And from now on you're just my ordinary dog and my ordinary bear, and I'm just ordinary me.'

'Woof,' said Bear the dog, and jumped up against Luka and licked his face. Luka hugged him tightly. 'After what you just did,' he said, 'I'll never let anybody think of dogs as bad-luck animals, because it was a lucky day for all of us when you became my dog.'

'Will somebody please tell me what is going on?' Soraya said faintly.

'It's okay, Mum,' said Luka, hugging her as tightly as he could. 'Calm down. Life is finally back to being ordinary again.'

'There's nothing ordinary about you,' his mother answered, kissing the top of his head. 'And, ordinary life? In this family, we know there's no such thing.'

On the flat roof of the Khalifa house, that cool evening, a dinner table was set out under the stars – yes, the stars had come out again! – and a feast was eaten, a feast of delicious slowly roasted meat and quickly pan-fried vegetables, of sour pickles and sweet-meats and cold pomegranate juice and hot tea, but also of some rarer foods and drinks – happiness soup, curried excitement and great-relief ice cream. At the very centre of the table, in their little Ott Pot, were the remaining five Ott Potatoes, glowing softly with the Fire of Life. 'So this other Soraya you became so fond of,' said Soraya Khalifa to Luka, just a little too sweetly, 'she said that if a healthy person eats one of these it can give them long life, and maybe even let them live for ever?'

Luka shook his head. 'No, Mum,' he said, 'it wasn't the Insultana of Ott who said that. It was Ra the Supreme.'

In spite of a life spent with the fabled Shah of Blah, Soraya Khalifa had never entirely liked this fanciful stuff, which she now had to put up with from both her sons as well as her storyteller husband. Tonight, though, she was making a real effort. 'And this Ra. . .' she began, and Luka finished the sentence for her, '. . . told me that personally, speaking in Hieroglyph, which was translated for me by a talking squirrel named Ratatat.'

'Oh, never mind,' said Soraya, giving up. 'All's well that ends well, and as for these so-called "Ott Potatoes", I'll just tuck them away in the pantry, and we can decide what to do with them on another day.'

Luka had just been wondering how it would be if he, his brother, his mother and his father could all live for ever. The idea struck him as more frightening than exciting. Maybe his dog Bear had been right, and it was better to do without Immortality, or even the possibility of it. Yes − maybe it would be better if Soraya hid the Ott Potatoes somewhere, so that all the Khalifas could slowly forget about their existence; and then maybe they, the Potatoes in their Pot, would finally get bored of waiting to be eaten, and would slip back across the Frontier into the World of Magic, and the Real World would be Real again, and life would be just that, life, and that would be more than enough.

The night sky was full of stars. 'As we know,' said Rashid Khalifa, 'sometimes the stars start dancing, and then anything can happen. But some nights it's good to see everything just staying put in its rightful place, so that we can all relax.'

'Relax my foot,' said Soraya. 'The stars may not be dancing, but we're certainly going to.'

She clapped her hands, and at once Dog the bear got up on his hind legs and began to stamp out the African Gumboot Dance, and Bear the dog jumped up and began to howl a Top Ten melody, and then the Khalifa family leapt to its feet and began to jig about energetically, and to join in the dog's song as well. And we'll leave them there, the rescued father, the loving mother, the older brother, and the young boy home from his great adventure, along with his lucky dog and his brotherly bear, up on the roof of their home on a cool night under the stationary, unchanging stars, singing and dancing.